CROW'S SCORN

USA TODAY BESTSELLING AUTHOR
MISTY WALKER

Crow's Scorn

Copyright © 2022 Misty Walker

Cover Design: Kate Farlow

Photographer: Xram Ragde

Editor: Novel Mechanic

Formatting: M Walker, LLC

ALL RIGHTS RESERVED. This book contains material protected under International and Federal Copyright Laws and Treaties. Any unauthorized reprint or use of this material is prohibited. No part of this book may be reproduced or transmitted in any form or by any means, electronic or mechanical, including photocopying, recording, or by an information and retrieval system without express written permission from the Author/Publisher.

This is a work of fiction. Names, characters, places, and incidents either are the product of the author's imagination or are used fictitiously, and any resemblance to actual persons, living or dead, business establishments, events, or locales is entirely coincidental.

I dedicate this book to Ariadna Basulto who constantly tells me how pretty and smart I am.

DIAMOND KINGS MC

Everything is bigger in Texas.
The men, their bikes, their guns and even their hearts.
On the biggest ranch in West Texas, you'll find the Diamond Kings MC.
A group of tough, growly bikers happy with their solitary existence.
Until love walks in and challenges them to the ultimate test.
It's time for them to man up and accept their fate or they'll lose their soulmates forever.

PROLOGUE
TALYNN, AGE 12

I sit at the top of the stairs, close enough to hear what's going on but not close enough to get caught. There's a fight going on downstairs, which often happens, but this one seems especially bad.

My brother, Henry, has really done it this time, and I'm scared for him. I don't understand why he can't stop getting in trouble. It seems simple. Follow the rules, and Momma and Daddy don't have a reason to yell.

"Your mom and I have discussed it, and we've decided. You're eighteen now, and school will be out in a few months. Since you don't have the grades to get into any college worth a damn, you have two options. Enlist or move out," Dad says in his cop voice, which is sterner than his normal voice.

"I'm not enlisting," Henry says with his whole chest.

"Then you better start looking for a job and an apartment because we won't have you causing chaos in this house anymore." Daddy's fist slams into the dining room table.

This is bad.

I startle when my other brother, Ben, crouches next to me. "Hey, squirt. What's going on?"

Ben is four years younger than Henry and is his opposite. He's quiet, shy, and smart. He wins all kinds of awards at school, and the entire town knows him and loves him.

"Mom and Dad are pissed," I say, even though pissed is a bad word.

Ben won't tell. He's a good brother and looks out for Henry and me.

"What did he do now?"

"Deputy Sterling brought him home tonight because Henry was tagging the Get Go. And he had drugs on him." My brow furrows. "What does enlist mean?"

"It's a verb meaning to enroll in the armed services." When he sees my confusion, he clarifies. "It means to join the military."

"Oh."

Ben sits next to me, bumping my shoulder with his. "It's gonna be okay. Henry'll calm them down like he always does."

We fall quiet when Henry yells, "You have to have credit to get an apartment!"

"Then find a roommate!" Daddy yells back.

"This is bullshit."

"Henry," Mom scolds.

Bullshit is a very bad word.

"You want me to live on the streets, fine. Good to know where I stand with y'all." The legs of a dining room chair screech, and Henry storms past the stairs and out the front door, slamming it for good measure.

"That went well," Ben says sarcastically.

I like sarcasm because I can say what I mean but play it off like it's a joke, and no one can get mad. Mom says it's passive-aggressive—whatever that means.

My lip trembles thinking about my brother living on the streets. "Will they kick him out?"

Ben ruffles my hair. "No. They just want him to grow up. It'll be okay."

I stare out my bedroom window doing what I do best—spying on my brothers in the backyard. My heart pitter-patters when Colton Masters joins them. Colt is Henry's best friend and my one true love.

I remember the day I realized I loved him. I was six, and Colt was ten. My parents were having a pool party to celebrate the beginning of summer and allowed my brothers and me to invite a friend. I invited my bestie, Sarah, and since Colt was both my brothers' best friend, they invited him.

Sarah and I were having a diving contest when I slipped on the diving board and hit my head as I fell in. I passed out, and when I woke up, I was in Colt's arms as he carried me out of the pool and over to the grass.

He smiled down at me, and it was all over.

I was his.

I've only been Henry and Ben's kid sister to him, but I started my period this year, and my boobs are coming in. It's only a matter of time before he realizes he loves me.

He's sixteen now, and he's changing too. Last month was Momma's annual pool party, and when Colt took his shirt off, he had muscles and hair in places that weren't there last summer. His voice is deeper now too.

He's the cutest boy in Diamond, and all the girls at our school are jealous because he hangs out at my house almost every day. Today is no different.

The three boys huddle in a circle. Henry pulls something out of the back of his pants, but I can't tell what it is. I catch a quick flash of silver but can't quite make out what it is.

Wanting to hear what they're saying, I carefully open my window. Sometimes it squeaks, and I don't want them to catch me and tattle to Momma.

"Put it back," Ben says. "It's dangerous."

"Don't be a pussy." This came from Henry, of course, because he has a potty mouth.

"I'm not a pussy."

"Let's take it to the hill," Colt says.

The three take off, and I'm on my feet in seconds. They don't know it, but I follow them all the time. Momma says I'm sneaky, and one day I'll see something I wish I hadn't, but she's wrong. I want to see and hear everything that involves Colton Masters.

Past the small patch of lawn and pool, our backyard is a whole lot of dirt, shrubs, and weeds. At the very edge of the property is a giant boulder big enough that Henry and his friends can hide behind it and get into trouble.

I wait until they round the rock and take off

running, keeping my steps light so they won't hear me coming. I'm almost there when a loud bang echoes through the air, freezing me in place. My heart races—not because I was running or from the excitement of spying on Colton. No. It's fear because I know that sound.

A gunshot.

Daddy is a Sheriff's Deputy and big on guns. He owns an entire arsenal of everything from hunting guns to handguns. He taught my brothers and me how to use them, but he knows better and keeps them locked in his garage safe.

My feet inch forward while my head screams to run the other way. My skin crawls, and my stomach turns, knowing whatever I'm about to see is bad. I didn't recognize the shiny silver thing Henry showed Ben and Colt before, but I do now.

I don't bother tiptoeing the way I usually do as I round the rock because the only sound I hear is my heart thumping in my ears. The boys aren't talking or joking or laughing like usual—another clue that whatever happened is bad.

What I see is so much worse than anything I could've imagined. My eyes land on Henry first. He's doubled over, his hands tugging on his hair, and his face is bright red. My gaze flicks to Colton, a haunted expression on his face and a silver gun resting in his open palms.

Then I see Ben lying on the ground, blood soaking the dirt under his head. His eyes are open, and there's a small, red hole in his forehead.

I scream. It's high-pitched and loud. A sound I've never made before, and I hope I never do again.

Mom was right. I saw something I wish I hadn't.

CHAPTER 1
CROW

Present day- twenty years later...

I pull up to the ranch in my piece of shit truck, same as I do every day, but today is different. Today, I don't have to report to my parole officer or take a piss test. And after I finish working, I don't have to go back to the halfway house to a creepy-ass roommate who likes to watch me sleep.

Parking in front of one of the cabins, I hop out and grab my cardboard box. All my earthly possessions are in it—some clothes and a couple books—but after owning nothing while I was behind bars, this box means the fucking world to me.

I find Ruin, our club president, standing outside my cabin.

"Crow," he says in greeting.

"Prez." I give him a chin lift.

He hands me a set of keys. "It's all yours."

"Thanks, brother." I take them and unlock the door.

Stepping inside, I look around. It's a simple one-bedroom cabin with minimal furniture, but for the first time in a long time, I have my own space.

Damn, it feels fucking amazing.

"Two years in juvie, thirteen in the state pen, and five years in that halfway house. . . it's probably weird to have all that behind you, huh?" Ruin asks.

"Real fuckin' weird," I admit.

"I'm glad it all worked out."

One of the terms of my parole was getting a job, but seeing how not a lot of businesses in this small town would hire a felon, pickings were slim. Until my PO found me a job as a hired hand at the Diamond Kings Ranch. I didn't know fuck all about animals, but Ruin hired me on the spot.

The ranch is owned by the Diamond Kings MC, who use it as a front to wash any money they make running guns. No one knows about that outside the club, though. Or if they do, they can't prove it.

When I first came to work here, I suspected there was more to them than riding bikes. But it wasn't until one year into my parole when the club approached me about prospecting that I knew for sure.

Joining an outlaw biker gang was obviously a violation of my parole, but I did it anyway and kept it on the down-low. After a year of prospecting, I patched in. Two years after that, I became the enforcer for the club.

I'd never say it out loud, but the club gave me back so much of what I lost while locked up. Pride, self-worth, and more than that, a family—given my parents abandoned me after I got sent away.

Not that I blame them. The whole town turned against them after the accident. Dad lost his law firm because no one wanted his representation, and Mom's friends avoided her.

I was only in juvie for a month when they came for visitation and told me they were leaving Diamond. They didn't outright say it was the last time I'd hear from them, but I knew. Dad couldn't look me in the eye, and Mom wouldn't stop crying.

The fucked-up part of the whole thing is they never once asked me what happened behind the rock that day. No one did. The truth didn't seem to matter to anyone. Talynn, Henry and Ben's little sister, told the law what she saw, and that was it. I became the most notorious villain in Diamond, Texas, and the judge threw the book at me.

"Oh, forgot to tell you. Your bike arrived this morning."

Like a kid on Christmas, I dash back outside and up to the garage. There, shiny and new, is my Harley Softail Cruiser. I saved every penny I could from each paycheck for this bike, and she's finally here.

I waste no time starting her up, noticing how different she feels from the 2008 Fat Bob I learned on.

"She's sick, huh?" Ruin shouts over the engine.

"I'm takin' her for a ride."

He motions down the drive, and I take off. Shaking my head in the wind, a stupid-ass grin spreads across my face as I speed down the road. There's no better feeling than a powerful engine between your legs and the danger of having nothing between you and the unforgiving road.

I ride for as long as I can, but I got a job to do, so I reluctantly pull back into the bike stall and park my main bitch.

"How'd she ride?" Ruin asks.

"Like a fuckin' dream."

He walks me back to my cabin but doesn't go in.

"I'll let you get settled," Ruin says. "See you later for church?"

"Yeah, Prez. Thanks."

I have a few minutes before I need to feed the horses, so I take a seat on the edge of the bed. Scrubbing a hand over my head, I try to make this real in my mind. It's not only having my own space. I've spent the last twenty years being watched, monitored, and surveilled, but now, I'm on my own.

Laughing to myself, I flop back on the bed. Shit. This feels good.

A knock has me sitting back up, wiping my grin away. "Yeah?"

The door opens, and Sin, the VP, walks in. "You settlin' in okay?"

"Yep. Probably need to run to the store for some shit, but I'm good."

"Happy to be done with all that legal shit?" he asks, knowing everything I've been through.

"Hell yeah," I admit. "Feels fuckin' awesome, brother."

"Hell yeah." He steps back onto the small porch. "Just came by to tell you Sugar's throwing a hissy fit."

I roll my eyes. "That cunt's needy."

Following him outside, we say our goodbyes, and

I head to the stables. I like to bitch about the horses, but I don't mean it. These horses saved my life, and I don't know where I'd be without this job that's turned into so much more.

"Heard you were bein' a bitch," I say to the brown Quarter Horse that's been on the ranch less time than I have.

She gives me a look I know means she wants a treat. I walk over to the bag of apples and hold one out to her. She takes it gently and munches while I grab a brush. I have stalls to muck and meals to prep, but I can take a minute for my favorite horse.

"I moved in," I say, brushing her down. "It's that cabin right over there. I know. Doesn't look like much, but you know me. Don't need much."

She whinnies in agreement.

"I'm officially off parole." A breeze blows through the stalls, causing Sugar's hair to fly into my mouth, and I spit and spatter until it's out. "Anyway, haven't heard from Mom or Dad. Thought since I was on the outside, they might reach out. But nope. Tried to call them but their numbers changed. Must've missed the letter tellin' me what the new ones are."

Sugar nuzzles under my arm, making me laugh.

"Yeah, you're right. I don't fuckin' need 'em. Sure would be nice to see a familiar face, though. Not just the ugly mugs of the bastards around here." I put the brush back on the shelf. "I got shit to do. Can't spend all day beautifyin' you."

She huffs, and I leave her to get going on the chores.

I'm fucking beat by the time I crawl into bed. A hard day's work will do that for a man. It's the best part of being out of prison. In there, I couldn't exhaust myself in a single hour of yard time. No matter how many laps I ran or how many reps I did with the weights, by the end of the night, I'd be pacing the cell, driving my cellmate crazy.

Now I get every ounce of my energy depleted, and it's from good work, honest work. Something Dad would've been proud of if he were still talking to me. He wouldn't have to know about the gun running.

It's been too dangerous for me to go on runs since I was on parole and could be stopped for any reason. But now that I'm free and clear, it's time for me to step up and get more involved. I'm fucking ready for it and the big paychecks it'll bring.

Stripping down, I turn the shower on hot. The spray feels fucking heavenly standing under it. I haven't had a hot shower in so fucking long. Not one. And I sure as shit haven't taken my time in the shower in as long. You're vulnerable when you're naked, and speaking from experience, it's no fun to be throwing punches with your cock flopping around.

Though, that's the most action my cock has seen in as many years. Daring to jack-off in bed put me in a more compromising position, so that didn't happen very often.

My dick twitches, and I shrug. Might as well. I'm alone and safe. Soaping up my hand, I fist my cock, my other hand pressed against the tile above my head. I conjure up images of chicks with big tits and bigger asses. I'm so pent up, I pity the first woman I unload on. She'll either get the ride of her life or a two-pump chump. Not sure yet.

I went to juvie before I had the chance to experience a woman. Something I wholeheartedly regret. Trisha Campbell was my girlfriend back then, and she let me feel her up and finger her, but that's the extent of my sexual experience.

The guys brag about the parties they throw and all the club sluts that hang around. Without a P.O. making sure I'm back at the halfway house after my shift, I'll be free to join in and finally get my dick wet. Being a virgin at my age is fucking pathetic and something I'd never admit to my brothers.

First order of business, get laid.

CHAPTER 2
TALYNN

Pulling up to Daddy's house, my heart sinks like it always does. While the lawn is mowed and the hedges are trimmed, Momma's flower boxes—ones that used to be full of beautiful flowers this time of year—sit empty, nothing but a few dead stems poking out of the dry dirt.

I offered to keep up her tradition and plant some annuals, but Daddy wouldn't hear it. He can't bear the idea of Momma not being the last person to touch those beds. And I get it. I miss her too. But it's been twenty years. It's time to move on.

"Daddy?" I call out as I walk through the door whose frame is notched with mine and my brothers' heights, starting from birth. I ghost my fingers over

Ben's last marker, taken when he turned fourteen. Even then, he was taller than I am now.

"In here."

I follow the voice to the den and find Daddy in his recliner, a beer wedged between his hip and the worn leather, holding up the newspaper. Yes, he still reads an actual newspaper, though our local paper added digital subscriptions ten years ago.

"I thought I'd grill up a steak and warm up those baked potatoes from last night." I kiss him on the cheek. "Sound good?"

"You don't have to come over here and make me dinner every night. I'm perfectly capable of—"

"Of what, Daddy? Warmin' up a microwave dinner?" I snicker. The man could burn water if left unsupervised. Momma kept very traditional roles in our house, so Daddy wasn't allowed to chop vegetables. Though he would've done anything for her.

"They make healthy TV dinners these days," he grumbles.

"I don't mind. It's not like I have anythin' else to do." My phone chimes, and I pull it out. My plant app reminds me which of my many plants need attention.

"Who needs what now?"

"Kathy. It's her day to get a neem oil mistin'."

"A what now?"

"Neem oil for spider mites."

"Well, now. See? You got other shit to do 'sides makin' your ol' man dinner." He gestures to my phone. "You have a plant most likely bein' overrun by spider mites."

"Hardy har har," I say sarcastically while clicking the "remind me again later" button because Kathy really does need that treatment.

I fire up the cast iron and set the oven to preheat before starting a quick steak rub.

"How was your shift today?" Daddy calls out.

"You know how it was, considerin' you're my boss and use that fact to spy on me."

"Just keepin' you safe."

Daddy is now the sheriff of Diamond, Texas, and I'm one of his few deputies. It's not the kind of job he wanted for me. He'd prefer me to be at home, married with babies by now. And since I turned thirty-two this year, he can literally hear my biological clock ticking.

It's so misogynistic, it makes me cringe. Though the thought of having babies doesn't make me squirm like it once did, I'd need a man in my life or the funds for fertility treatments. Neither of which I currently have.

"That scuffle at the Get Go was a doozy," I say.

"Cal needs to learn to let things go," Daddy grumbles.

The smallish fight was the most excitement I had today, and it was over the perfect pack of strawberries. The two old men nearly came to fisticuffs.

"I don't know. I'm on Mr. Smith's side. He makes a better homemade jam, so I think he should've had his pick of berries."

I work fast, searing the meat and preparing the toppings for the potatoes. Plating the meals, I place Daddy's on a TV tray since it's time for *Jeopardy* and take mine to the table.

"Had something I wanted to talk to you about," Daddy says.

"What's up?"

He gets out of his recliner and joins me at the table. Uh-oh. This is serious.

"I don't want you to freak out—"

"Is it Henry? Is he okay?" My heart sinks to the freaking floor. Anytime Daddy wants to talk to me about something, it typically involves Henry getting busted on drug charges or calling to ask for money.

"No, it's not him. Not this time, anyway. It's something else."

"Spit it out, Daddy."

"Colton Masters is back in town." He winces, knowing what that news will do to me, and I don't disappoint.

Pushing back from the table, I stand. "What? How could you let that happen?"

"Calm down, Talynn. He has every right to live here, even if we don't want him to. He served his time and didn't have so much as alcohol in his piss the whole five years of his parole. I know because I've been watchin' him."

"There must be a way we can get him out. No one wants him here." Angry tears burn my eyes, and I furiously wipe them away, not wanting to give that man another minute of my time. How quickly my mood can change. "Where's he livin'?"

"I'm not tellin' you."

"Why?" I demand.

"Because I know you, and you'll march your butt over there and make his life hell."

"Of course I will." I huff. "And he deserves every minute of it."

"Now, Tal—"

"No, Daddy. Don't do that. He ruined our lives. Not just Ben's. *All* of our lives." My eyes flick to the portrait above the river rock fireplace. It's the last one we took as a whole family.

"I'm up for reelection this year. Can't have my daughter out there breakin' laws in some sort of revenge scheme."

"You're wrong. If we drove him out of town, your reelection would be in the bag." I scrape my plate into the trash, appetite gone.

"Sit down and talk about this." Daddy's sheriff voice comes out, which would usually stop me in my tracks. But not now. Not with this news.

"I'm fine. Swear it."

"You're not fine, and I'm worried about you leaving in such a tizzy."

"I'll go home. I promise."

"You better."

I kiss his cheek. "I will."

Getting in my squad car, I head out to my first order of business for the day.

I did go home last night, but only to plot. After calling around, I found out Colton is living on the Diamond Kings Ranch with all the other lowlifes of

Diamond. Course he is. It's where he belongs if he belonged in this town at all, which he doesn't.

There might've been a time when hearing Colton's name would send me in a downward spiral, and I'd lock myself in my house to cry and scream. But I'm not that woman anymore. Now, all I feel is rage and the need for vengeance.

Skidding to a stop in front of the Diamond Kings Ranch with my lights flashing, I hop out and march over to the first person I see. He's tall, muscled, covered in tattoos, and has a trimmed beard. If I didn't know he was part of the club, I might consider him good-looking. Sexy, even.

"Which one does Colton Masters stay in?" I point to the collection of cabins the gang members live in. And yes, I said gang because the Diamond Kings MC is no more a club than a tiger is a pussy cat.

"Who?" asks the man whose vest patch reads Sin.

"Colton Masters," I repeat but slower this time.

His brows knit together in confusion. "You mean Crow?"

These assholes are always giving themselves nicknames. Crow is close to Colton, so I nod.

"That one." He points to a cabin on the west side of the property.

"Thanks."

"But you can't—"

I don't stick around for the rest of that because, yes, I can. I talked a judge into giving me a search warrant this morning. I might've exaggerated the circumstances, but I'll talk my way out of it if anyone questions me.

Jiggling the door handle, I find it locked, but that doesn't stop me. I take a few steps back and throw my shoulder into it, smiling when it crashes open.

"There." I dust my hands off and step inside.

It's a shit hole with nothing but a futon in the living area, a small galley kitchen and breakfast nook with a two-person table and chair set, a bathroom, and a bedroom with only a bed and a dresser. I start in the living room, tossing the mattress off the futon and slashing through it with my knife, sending fiberfill all over the ground.

I'd be thankful if drugs or guns popped out, but I doubt they're dumb enough to leave evidence of their criminal activities lying around. That's not the point of this mission.

In the kitchen, I toss every dish, cup, and pan onto the floor before emptying the drawers. My fuel-filled rage doesn't stop when I reach the bedroom. I finish emptying the top drawer when I hear shouting from outside.

"What the fuck is going on?" a deep voice booms. I vaguely recognize it though it's more mature now. But it has the same rasp I remember from when I was twelve and thought Colton Masters hung the moon.

I pull the warrant from my pocket and unfold it, waiting for him to barge in here and argue with me. A man steps inside looking spitting mad, and I freeze.

Colton grew up. He's taller and, my God did the boy fill out.

His once teenage physique morphed into a manly one, judging by the way his shirt stretches across his muscled chest. He has a tapered waist, and his jeans hug solid thighs in a way that tells me this man is strong and powerful.

The same brown eyes I remember from before stare back at me, but a lot about his face has changed. He now has scruff that's not long enough to be a beard but longer than a five o'clock shadow and worry lines between his brow that are bunched together as he glares at me angrily.

"I have a warrant." I shove the paper in his face after regaining my faculties.

He snags it from my hand, his face turning an ugly shade of red as he looks at the mess I've created. "Suspicion of drugs in the home of a known felon? Where did this suspicion come from? Because the only drug I've ever done was smokin' skunky weed with my best friend when I was sixteen, and I'm still not sure it wasn't oregano."

"I don't write the warrants. I only serve 'em."

He doesn't know who I am; this I know for sure. At least not yet. But he's about to. I watch as his gaze lowers from my face to my gold name tag that reads Dep. Davis. His eyes go wide and settle back on my face.

"Talynn?" he croaks out.

"Deputy Davis," I correct with my chin held high. "Now make my life easier and tell me where the drugs are. We both know I'll find 'em." I move to the second drawer and dump it at his feet.

It's a lie. I haven't even found a cigarette, let alone dope. But if I'm in for a penny, I'm in for a pound.

He sinks onto the bed, running a dirty hand through his hair. Does he think this display of emotion will make me feel sorry for him? Hell, no. This man should've spent the rest of his miserable life in prison. Accident or not, my brother is dead.

"I knew there was a chance I'd run into you, but I didn't think it would happen like this," he says quietly.

"Would you rather take me off guard as we both reached for a cucumber at the Get Go?"

"No." His bushy brows furrow. "I had plans to come talk to you. Tell you I was back, but I guess"—he blows out a breath—"I thought I had more time before word got out I was livin' here."

"Word's out, asshole, and just so you know, the entire town wants you gone. So, do us all a favor and get the hell outta Diamond." I move into the bathroom and dump a toiletry bag on the small vanity.

Colton stays put, not saying a word but tracking me with those brown eyes that now look tired and sad.

After looking in the cabinet under the sink, in the shower, and in the toilet tank, I turn in a circle and realize there's nowhere else to look. My rampage is over.

Stalking over to Colton, I point a finger in his face. "We've got our eyes on you. If you so much as take a shit wrong, I'll know about it."

"I can call you and tell you every time my stomach grumbles, if it'd make it easier." The corner of his lip curves up a hair, which pisses me off even more.

"You think this is funny?" I burn him with my glare. "You killed the sweetest boy on the planet, drove your best friend to drugs and alcohol, and sent the woman you called your second mom into an early grave. You think *that's* funny?"

His face falls, and a certain amount of satisfaction fills me.

CHAPTER 3
CROW

I frown, all trace of humor gone. "What'd you say?"

"Which part? The part where you basically killed off half my family?"

"Your mom," I say, my throat constricting. "She's gone?"

"Yeah. Died of broken heart syndrome. Fittin', right?"

"Fuck," I curse, resting my head in my hands. I hadn't heard about that. Why would I have, though? Everyone stopped talking to me after that day. Even my own family. "And Henry?"

"Lives on the streets of Dallas, last I heard. Only a matter of time before your actions will be responsible for his death too." Her tone drips with condescension and hurt. I don't say shit about it. I deserve whatever she dishes out.

"Fuck," I say again.

"Yeah, fuck. So if you could just move far, far away from here, that'd be great." She storms out, stepping around the door she knocked off its hinges. Seconds later, her tires are kicking up gravel as she speeds off.

Sin walks in with a whistle. "What was that about?"

"The reason I went to prison."

"Well, shit. Need help cleaning up?"

"Nah, bro. I got this." I stand and clap him on the shoulder. "Sorry about the heat. Won't happen again."

"I saw the look in that woman's eyes. This is only beginning."

He's right, and it's naïve of me to think otherwise. This isn't going away, but I get an idea that might show Talynn a gesture of goodwill.

"Is it okay if I take off for a few days?" I ask.

"Don't see why not. We'll make sure the horses are taken care of."

Guilt hits me at leaving them for a while.

When I first got the job as a ranch hand, I was a fish out of water. Took me some time to find my place with the horses, and I was as skittish, scared, and untrusting as they were. I'd been in prison longer than I'd been out, so not having the structure and social hierarchy I was used to was a difficult transition.

Slowly, the horses and I learned to trust each other, and now they really are my best friends. Even more so than my brothers, though I'm still tight with them.

"Yeah, okay."

I take the exit for the Dallas airport and unroll the window of my pickup. I'd rather be riding my new Harley, but if I find Henry, I'll need a way to get him back to Diamond.

I stopped at a diner for breakfast before starting my search. The waitress clued me in on the areas of the city that have the highest homeless population. I checked out a few of them yesterday and am continuing my search today. It feels like searching for a needle in a haystack but something in me believes I'll find him.

Turning into the neighborhood the waitress told me about, I expected a couple encampments but what

I find is so much worse. Tents lining the roads, trash everywhere, and a stench of piss permeating the air.

This could've been me if I hadn't found the Diamond Kings, and I wouldn't be surprised if some of the same faces I was in prison with were living here.

Society doesn't give a shit about felons. Most of us only want what everyone does—respect, a decent job that pays enough to keep the lights on, and freedom. But the second we're released from prison, we're given a few bucks and a bus ticket. Those don't last long, and it sure as shit won't get a person on their feet.

I lucked out, and I thank the Lord above for where I landed.

Deciding I won't find Henry driving around, I park the truck on the side of the road and set off on foot, my folding Spyderco knife in my pocket. I have a deep distrust of everyone, something instilled in me the day I went to juvie. Though some of that is fading, I revert to the kid I was back then when I'm in a new situation.

Being a felon, I shouldn't carry any kind of weapon, but I haven't seen a cop yet, so I'm not too worried.

I approach a man sitting outside of a tent, peeling

an orange. "Hey, man. I'm lookin' for someone. Name is Henry."

I wish I had a picture, but the only ones I have are from news articles about the shooting. I doubt he looks the same as when he was eighteen, but I show it to him anyway.

"No. Haven't seen him." He tosses the peel onto the street.

"He's an addict. Anywhere I might find a guy like that?"

"There's an abandoned building 'round the corner. Might be there."

"Thanks." I tuck my phone and cross through the alley.

I look up and down the road until I spot a three-story brick building that has seen better days. It has boarded-up windows, and the house numbers are falling off. That must be it.

The hairs on the back of my neck stand on end as I climb through a window. This place has an eerie feel and smells like piss and rotten food. There's a worn sofa to my left—if you can still call it that—with the cushions missing, so it's nothing but torn fabric and springs now.

There's shit everywhere. Trash, used needles, clothes, and a whole lot of stuff I can't pinpoint.

Graffiti covers the walls with everything from prayers to pictures of evil-looking demons. Mixed crowd.

Thinking about Henry living here makes me sick. This isn't how it was supposed to be. Right before the accident, he told me he was making changes. He planned to visit the Army recruitment center and join up. He wanted to make his folks proud of him for once.

I walk through that room and down the hall to inspect the rest of the main floor. The first room I come to has an executive-style desk sitting in front of a window. There's a filing cabinet in the corner and random papers scattered on the floor. Before being abandoned, this place must've been an office building of some sort.

"What do you want?" a raspy voice asks, and I nearly jump out of my skin. I hadn't seen him sitting in the corner. He's older and clearly a user, judging by his facial ticks, black nubs for teeth, and the way he's rolling his head on his neck.

"I'm looking for someone. You know a guy named Henry?"

"Know a lot of guys named Henry."

"This one is in his late thirties. I got a picture, but it's old." When I took a screenshot of the family portrait the news article used, I zoomed in on his smiling face.

"I might know him," he says, chin lifted high.

I fish a twenty out of my wallet. "Maybe this'll jog your memory." I hate contributing to his addiction, but he's going to get his fix one way or another. Might as well make today easy on him.

"He comes by sometimes. Doesn't stay here, though."

"Have you seen him today?"

"Yeah, not too long ago. Might still be upstairs."

"Thanks." Hope fills me, and I quickly find the stairs.

The same amount of disarray is on the second level, but I find more than I bargained for on the third level. People are passed out, sitting with their back against the walls, surrounded by drug paraphernalia. I spot a group of younger guys playing cards. Their game comes to a halt when they see me. These are the ones supplying the dope.

None of them look like Henry. Though I don't know what he looks like anymore, I'd recognize him if I saw him. For ten years, we spent every minute we weren't sleeping or in school together.

"Need something, friend?" one of the men calls out.

"No, just lookin' for someone."

"Not the kind of place you want to hang out in, if you know what I mean."

I nod, knowing I've overstayed my welcome, and make my way back to the stairs and out of the building. Part of me is glad I didn't find Henry in that place, and another is disappointed. I hoped I could bring him home, show Talynn there's still some good in me. That's not the only reason though. Despite what Talynn thinks, I care that my childhood best friend is suffering.

Does she know he came to see me when I landed in the pen? He only showed once, and the visit was painful and taxing. I was glad he never showed up again, but it makes me wonder if I could've stopped him from this life had he come to visit more often.

There's an alley in the back of the building, which I decide to check before I head home. Shoving my hands in my pockets, I lift my shoulders to my ears to appear less of a threat as I step into the alley. A few abandoned dumpsters overflow with trash, but otherwise, it appears empty.

I almost turn to leave when a sound catches my attention. It's a pained cry—animal or human—I don't fucking know.

I cautiously step further into the alley, checking

behind the first dumpster and seeing nothing. The sun is going down, and the alley is narrow, making it dark enough back here to make me uncomfortable, but I keep going.

On the back side of the second dumpster is the source of the noise. A man is on the ground, and he's in a bad way. His eyes are blackened and swollen, his lip is split open, and a gash on his forehead is gushing blood.

Fuck.

"You okay?" I ask.

"Fine. Just fine," he slurs.

Then I notice the needle still dangling from his thin arm.

"Let's get you some help." I crouch down and use my shirt to cover my fingers to pull the syringe from his arm and toss it on the ground. I do the same for the rubber tourniquet before holding my hand out to him. "Come on. You need a hospital."

"Nah, man. I'm good."

Motioning to his forehead, I say, "Judgin' but that cut, you need a few stitches, at least."

"No hospital," he mutters, his eyes rolling into his head.

I slap his cheek, rousing him. "You got somewhere I can take you? Where are you stayin'?"

"There." He lifts a finger at the abandoned building.

He'll contract an infection or overdose before morning in the state he's in, but I don't know what the hell to do with him other than drop him off at a hospital.

"What's your name?" I ask.

"Henry," he slurs.

I stumble back, staring at him with new eyes and trying to connect similar features to the kid I used to know. He has the same dirty blond hair, though instead of the buzz cut his mama used to enforce on him, it's shaggy and tangled. He's about the same height, though it's hard to tell with him sitting down.

There's one way I can know for sure if this is the man I came looking for, so I squat down and lift his shirt up. There, across his ribs, is a long, white scar. He got that from jumping Mr. White's fence when we were eleven years old. We thought it was a genius idea to piss off his bull and see if we could outrun him. We did, in fact, outrun him, but the barbed fence caught Henry on his way over and tore right through him. He got twenty-five stitches and was grounded for two weeks for that stunt.

"You're the dumbass I was lookin' for," I say and

toss the fucker over my shoulder, ignoring his protests.

He weighs next to nothing, a byproduct of filling his arm instead of his belly, and he smells bad enough to gag a maggot.

Holding my breath, I carry him to my truck and deposit him in the front seat. I step up on the running board and pull the seatbelt over him, clicking it in place. All the while, he whines and complains but is too weak to get anywhere with it.

"You sit there and shut up," I say, hopping down.

"Where are we goin'?"

"Home."

CHAPTER 4
TALYNN

"Why are you so dramatic?" I ask Agatha, my fiddle-leaf fig. She's one of my newer plants, and despite all warnings from the shop owner, I thought I could give such a temperamental plant a good home. I was wrong. "I love you, Agatha. Why isn't that enough?"

I give her a good watering and move on to my happier plants. The ones who actually want to survive.

Momma was a plant lover, and after she died, I took them all in so Daddy didn't have to worry. Turns out, I'm pretty good at it, which makes me feel like I'm carrying on her legacy.

My chest constricts with the pain of her loss. Seeing Colton again stirs up all the old emotions and anger I thought I had dealt with. But I guess not because I haven't slept much in the two days since Daddy told me the news.

I thought tossing his place would make me feel better, but it didn't. There must be something else I can do to drive him out of Diamond without losing my job or getting in trouble with Daddy.

Once everyone has had their morning drink, I make myself a dippy egg and toast, settling onto my cute, vintage '60s dinette set. The top is a yellow swirl Formica, rimmed with chrome and matching vinyl chairs. The morning sun through the wall-to-wall windows covering the back of my house warms my skin and makes me happy as I eat my breakfast.

Looking around my tiny home, I'm proud of everything I've accomplished. Daddy thought I was crazy buying this place. Not only because of its size —one bedroom, one bathroom, and a loft—but also because it was a fixer-upper.

Over the last five years, I've replaced the floors and windows and remodeled the bathroom and kitchen. At this point, I've put more money into it than it's worth, but it has the cutest covered front porch that overlooks Mr. White's pastures, and the backyard is big enough for a dog someday.

I can still hear Daddy asking me how I expect to

raise a family in this small of a home, but that isn't even on my radar. I've dated my way through most of Diamond's eligible bachelors within a ten-year age gap, and not one of them ever made me want to marry them.

At this point in my life, I'm happy with my plants and the possibility of a dog in the future.

A knock at my door startles me from my thoughts. It's not unusual for someone to pop by because Diamond is a place where neighbors still ask for a cup of sugar but not typically this early in the morning.

Tightening my robe, I peer through the peephole to see Colton Masters standing on my porch. But he's not alone; he's holding up another man. I can't tell who because he's hunched forward, his head down.

What the hell?

I check to make sure my gun is in the drawer of my entry table, then unlock and open the door.

"Can we come in?" Colt's raspy voice is hoarser than it was the other day.

"What's this about?" I ask, not wanting to get involved with whatever this is.

"I found Henry."

Oh my God.

I throw my door open wide and take Henry's other

arm, helping to get him inside. "Take him to the sofa."

We release Henry to the couch, and I get the first look at my brother in over seven years. Daddy saw him last year after Henry served a six-month sentence for drugs. He tried to take him to rehab, but Henry wouldn't go. He jumped out of Daddy's truck at a stoplight and took off.

As far as I know, that's the last he's heard of my stupid, self-destructive older brother. Henry took Ben's death so hard, and he's been punishing himself ever since. It might've been Colt who shot Ben, but it was Henry who stole one of Daddy's guns and took it out to the rock that day. He's never forgiven himself.

"Where was he?" I sit next to Henry and lift his head up, shocked to see a three-inch gash across his forehead, a split lip, and black eyes. He's conscious but clearly high, judging by his glazed-over eyes.

"Dallas," Colt says.

"Why?" I don't want to sound appreciative, after all, he's the reason my brother was out there in the first place, but I can't help it. I'm so thankful to see Henry in flesh and blood. Even if he does look awful.

"Why what?"

"Why did you go lookin' for him?"

"Didn't like the idea of him bein' out there alone."

He shrugs. "Found him last night, but he was. . . in a bad way. Took him to a hotel for the night, wantin' to sober him up. Then this morning, he locked himself in the bathroom and"—he motions to Henry's current state—"by the time I jimmied the door open, he was like this again."

"How did you know where I lived?" I ask, accusation in my tone. I don't like that he knows any personal details about me. I don't trust him or his motives.

"It's Diamond," he says by way of explanation.

"Right." He'd only have to ask the clerk at the Get Go to find out. People around here are trusting. Too trusting, apparently. "Can you get the first aid kit in my bathroom? It's around the corner."

"Sure." He disappears for way too long. I start to wonder what he's doing and regret sending him to nose through my house, but then he's back, first aid kit in hand. "This is your place, huh?"

"Yeah." I snatch the red box from his hand and open it up, laying out all the supplies I need to clean up Henry's face.

"It looks like you." He tucks his hands in his pockets, looking around.

"You don't know me," I bite out.

"It looks like who you were," he corrects.

"And who was I?" I'm being a bitch, but I couldn't care less. No part of me wants this man near my family. Not anymore.

"You always liked old stuff." He motions to the turntable I keep next to the sofa. "Like the record player you drove us crazy with listenin' to Elvis Presley and Ray Charles. And those bell-bottom jeans with the daisy pattern bleached into them." He lifts a chin at my daisy print curtains. "You always were an old soul."

"Yeah, well, some of us don't change." I stand, moving to the door. "Listen, thanks for bringin' Henry here, but it's time for you to go."

"All right." He follows me to the door but stops on the porch, turning to face me. "If you need any help with him, you know where to find me."

The rage I felt when I found out he was back in town returns full steam. "Do you think this absolves you? That you can bring me my druggie brother, and all will be forgotten?" I scoff. "You killed Ben. There is *nothin'* you can do to make us forgive you. You get that, right?"

He hangs his head, and his hands go into his pockets. "Guess not."

He turns on his heels and gets inside an old,

orange pickup with chipped paint and rusty wheel wells.

Good riddance.

Closing the door, I return to Henry, who's now snoring. Cleaning up his face, I whisper all the things I've wanted to tell him over the last seven years about my house, plants, Daddy, job, everything. He sleeps through it all, and after I get him fixed up, I lift his feet onto the couch and rest his head on a pillow.

"We'll talk more when you wake up," I whisper.

It's my day off, so while Henry sleeps, I do laundry, clean, and sit in the big comfy chair in my room to read a book. I'm obsessed with historical romance, and the built-in bookcase in my room is full of them. Once a year, I go to Diamond's town-wide rummage sale and stock up.

Afternoon comes, and I pick up my cellphone to make the call I've been putting off all day.

"Hey, honey," Daddy answers.

"Hey. I was wonderin' if you'd come to my house for dinner tonight."

"I told you, I can feed myself—"

"That's not why. I have a visitor I think you'll want to spend time with." I chew on a fingernail.

"Who's that? You finally find yourself a man to give me some grandbabies?" He chuckles.

"No. Henry's home."

"What?"

"He's been sleepin' all day, but I'm sure he'll wake up soon, and when he does, I could use some reinforcements."

He blows out a breath. "Yeah, okay. I'll be right over."

"Daddy?" I croak.

"What, baby?"

"He's not well."

"I figured. Don't you worry about a thing. I'm loadin' up now."

"Okay." I hang up and brush a lone tear that streaks down my cheek. I've cried more times than I can count over Henry's addictions. It took a long time before I accepted that there was nothing I could do to help him. But having him here has me doubting that.

There must be something I can say or do to convince him to get help.

Hearing my antique couch squeak, I get up and go to the living room. Henry is stretched out, arms over his head, his eyes blinking open.

"Hey," I say.

He startles and sits up, his gaze suddenly clear. "Talynn? How the hell. . .?"

He looks around, only now noticing he's in my

house. He curses and runs a hand over his matted hair.

"Colt brought you to my house," I say.

"I thought that was a dream." He stands and moves to the door. "I can't be here."

Frantic, I grab his arm. "Please, Henry. Stay. For a while. Looks like you could use a shower and some clean clothes."

"So you can judge me and make me feel like shit for how I live my life? Hell no." He jerks his arm from my hold and opens the door.

"Where do you think you're goin'?" Daddy says, striding up the walk.

"Seriously? You called him?" Henry lands his accusing gaze on me.

"We love you and want to see you get better."

"Get better? This isn't a disease, Tal."

"It *is* a disease," I say. "There are doctors who can help."

"Okay, okay. Let's calm down for a second." Daddy steps inside. "We don't need to get into all that right now. Let's focus on gettin' you cleaned up and some food in your belly. Don't need to make it any more complicated than that right now."

Henry's shoulders slump. "Fine, but after that, I'm outta here."

"That's good." Daddy pulls him in for a hug that Henry doesn't return. "Nice to see you, Son."

"You too, Pops." He pulls away. "Where's the bathroom?"

"Right around the corner. There are fresh towels under the sink. Toss your clothes in the hall, and I'll get them in the wash. I have some of your old things in the attic, so I can find you something to wear. Might be too big on you now, but it'll do," I say.

"You kept my shit?"

"Some of it."

He nods and walks into the bathroom.

Daddy and I sit, not saying a word until the shower starts, the door opens, and clothes land on my hardwood.

"What are we going to do?" I ask.

"I'm gonna go up in your attic an' find him clothes while you get to work making him some supper."

"That's not what I meant. How are we gonna to get him into rehab?"

"We've had this discussion, Talynn. We can't talk him into doing anything he doesn't want to do. We've tried that, and it doesn't work."

"So you're going to let him leave after he eats?"

"If that's what he wants."

Irritation bubbles under my skin. He's given up. Not that I can blame him. I thought I had, too. But having him here changes things. I can't ignore what's right in front of my face.

Daddy heads to my laundry room, where the attic access is, and with no other choice, I go to the kitchen. Today was grocery shopping day, but since I didn't get that done, there's not a lot to choose from.

Opening my fridge, I find some carrots, celery, and half an onion. There's also half a roasted chicken. I can make chicken noodle soup, heavy on the noodles since that's all I have in abundance.

I fill the pot with water and add enough bullion to make it taste good, then get started on chopping vegetables. At one point, I hear Daddy hand Henry clothes. I'm glad I stopped him from tossing them out. A couple years after Momma died, he packed up everything that belonged to her, Ben, and Henry and only kept a few things that reminded him of them. I took most of what was left.

Knowing they were things Momma and Ben had touched at some point, I couldn't let them go. As far as Henry's stuff, I held out hope he'd return to us someday.

Henry enters the kitchen, looking clean but no less sickly. His eyes are sunken in despite the swelling, his hair is thin and brittle, and he probably weighs less than I do, though I'm a good foot shorter than him.

"Hey, Tal. Thanks for the shower. I feel like a new man." His smile is small and hesitant.

"Of course."

Daddy sits down at the dinette, and the three of us make small talk while I cook, not touching on anything too heavy. Once dinner is ready, we sit down as a family. Henry has three bowls of soup, eating like he hasn't had a meal in a long time. It hurts my heart knowing he probably hasn't.

"That was good." Henry pushes his bowl away and leans back.

"Thanks."

"Sure was." Daddy stands, setting his bowl in the sink. "I better get going. It was good to see you, Son."

Henry stands, and they hug. I can't believe Daddy's going to let him disappear again. Just because our previous attempts to help Henry haven't worked doesn't mean we should give up completely. There must be something we can do; something we haven't tried yet.

"Hey, Pops. Do you have some cash so I can catch a bus back to Dallas?"

Daddy flips through his wallet. "Sorry. I'm fresh out."

It's a lie. Daddy must've emptied his wallet before he got here because he always keeps a few hundred on hand. He doesn't believe in debit cards—something about the government tracking his spending. Henry must not remember this fact because he doesn't question him.

"Shit. Talynn? What about you?"

"I don't keep cash anymore. Not since I got my debit card." This is also a lie because though I don't think the government cares about what I buy, I keep a couple hundred like Daddy taught me.

"Can you go to the bank?" he asks.

"It's a Sunday. Banks aren't open," Daddy says.

"You can stay the night, and I'll get some cash tomorrow." I stand, taking mine and Henry's bowls to the sink, finally understanding Daddy's game. If we give him reasons to stay, he can't leave.

Henry sighs, and I don't miss his jerky movements and the sweat glistening on his brow. The withdrawal is kicking in. "I guess."

Daddy kisses the top of my head. "Sleep well."

"Thanks. You too."

He winks affectionately but his eyes are tight with concern. We both know I'm in for a rough night.

CHAPTER 5
CROW

I lie awake on my lumpy mattress, thinking about Henry and Talynn.

It's not that I expected her to change her tune because I brought her brother home, but I thought her icy demeanor might melt a little.

It made me happy seeing the home she's made for herself. I can't believe little Talynn is all grown up and shit. She was a cute kid and has turned into a beautiful woman.

It makes me an asshole for noticing how her curves came in, given the situation. But her cotton robe didn't hide much, and since I still haven't gotten laid, I'm wound tighter than a clock.

Her tits are more than a handful, and despite her trim waist, her round ass and thick thighs are things men like me dream of. Her tan skin glows, and her brown hair—in a tight bun when she tossed my cabin—is long and glossy.

Does she remember how she used to have a crush on me? Henry would tease me after finding pieces of scrap paper with her first name and my last name scribbled in her handwriting. She followed us around, spying on us, though she wasn't very good at it.

My stomach sinks when I remember how she found us that day. Would things have been different if she hadn't been there?

Probably not.

I can blame everyone who played a part in how things went down, but the truth is, I had my reasons for keeping quiet. If I knew then what I know now, things might've gone differently. But they didn't, and I thought I was doing what was best.

I fall asleep, reminding myself it's all over. I'm a free man and still have a whole life to live. That thought comforts me as I finally drift off.

It feels like my alarm goes off the second my eyes close, and I punch my pillow, pissed at how much today will suck on no sleep.

Getting up, I flip on the coffee maker. Tank, the club's Road Captain, showed me how to use it. I put one of the pods in the machine and press a button, allowing steamy, delicious coffee to sputter out and into my travel mug. Technology has changed since my Dad's old Mr. Coffee brewer.

I take my first sip and look out the window, the small blue seashell soap on the sill catching my eye. I pick it up and roll it around in my hand. I don't know why I took it from Talynn's bathroom when I got the first aid kit. It was stupid. She's been nothing but cold and cruel, but back when we were young, she was like my little sister too, and I guess I wanted something to remind me of who we once were to each other.

She's collected damn seashell soap since the first time her family took a trip to the ocean when she was five. She brought back a bag of them and gave me one. Her family took that same trip every year from then on, and every year, she'd give me stinky seashell soap.

My collection is probably sitting in a landfill somewhere, but it made me sentimental to see she's still collecting them. She had a huge ass jar sitting on a shelf next to a picture of the five of them on the beach. Judging by appearances, it was probably the last one they ever took as a family.

So much was destroyed by that accident. A one-second blip of time and *poof.* Everything changed.

After a quick shower, I get dressed in jeans, a T-shirt, and boots and head out for work. Taking care of the horses isn't difficult and doesn't require much of a uniform.

I make the rounds feeding everyone breakfast. Once that's done, I let them out into the pasture to graze while I clean out the stalls, and I'm done until later when I round everyone up for dinner and a groom. Usually, I take that time to eat some lunch and maybe grab a nap, but I got an idea while I was shoveling shit, so instead, I exchange my work boots for my riding boots and take off on my new Harley.

I don't know if Henry is still at Talynn's house, but if he is, he's probably sobered up, and it's high time we did some talking.

I do a drive-by first, making sure Talynn isn't home. When I don't see her Chevy Caprice in the drive, I flip around and park on the street. Keeping my eyes peeled, I walk up the drive and knock on the door.

Henry answers, looking a bit better than before, which isn't saying much because he looked like death run over the last time I saw him.

"Hey," I start, rubbing the back of my neck awkwardly. "Your sister home?"

"No, she's at work."

"Mind if I come in to talk?"

"Sure." He watches me curiously as I step inside.

"How are you doin'?" I ask.

He guides me to the living room and motions to a sofa covered in blankets and pillows. I push them aside and take a seat.

"I'm all right. Itchin' to get outta here." He sits down next to me.

"You leavin' already?"

"Yeah. I gotta get back. Got some jobs waitin' on me." He's lying. There are no jobs. He's jonesing for a fix. I can see it in his jumpy motions and how he's scratching at his arms.

"I see. Well, I'm glad I caught you before you left."

"What for?"

"It's been a while. Thought we could catch up," I say.

"Why? So you can tell me what a disappointment I am? Remind me of what you did and how I'm wastin' my second chance at life?"

"Well, yeah. I guess that covers it." I couldn't have said it better myself. I'm pissed at him for being such a fucking idiot.

"Well, save it. You can't say anythin' I don't already know."

"Then isn't it time to make a change? Seems like Talynn wants you here. Why don't you stick around a while and see what happens?" I ask.

"I'm a drug addict, Colt. I can't stay here. Only reason I haven't left yet is that Talynn refuses to go to the bank until after work." He finds a scab on his upper arm and picks relentlessly until it's bleeding.

"You don't have to be. I'm sure your old man and Talynn would get you into a place. You can beat this and take control of your life again."

"How inspirational," he bites out.

"I'm bein' serious here, Henry. If you don't owe it to yourself, you owe it to me. And you owe it to Ben."

At the mention of his younger brother, he deflates and wraps his arms around himself. "I am what I am because of Ben."

"No, you are what you are because you're weak." It's time for some tough love because whatever coddling Talynn's been doing isn't working.

"You're an asshole."

"Not the first time someone's called me that."

"I think it's best you go now."

"Nope." I get comfortable, throwing my arms around the back of the chair. "I want you to tell me why you won't even try."

"I have tried. I've been sober. Each time I get locked up, I suffer. And I'm not talkin' about coming off the drugs. I'm talkin' about the pain that eats me alive over what happened that day. I can't take it. I'd rather be high and living on the streets than feel that."

His honesty tears a hole through my heart. No one knows that pain like I do. The only difference is I couldn't escape it by sticking a needle in my arm. I had to go through it alone and scared with no loving family to support me the way Henry has.

"That's bullshit, and you know it. If you hadn't shoved all that shit down deep and covered it up with a needle in your arm, you'd be a different man today. That kind of pain don't last forever, but you gotta feel it first. You gotta go through the process until you can forgive yourself."

"Like you did?" One of his patchy brows lifts. "Because I see that look in your eyes. It's the same sorry, sad look I have."

"I'm workin' on it, unlike you. I got my freedom, I got my club, and I got a purpose. It might not be sunshine and rainbows yet, but at least I'm tryin'."

His eyes water, and my stomach sinks. "I don't know how."

I stand and tug him to his feet before wrapping him up in a hug. I haven't given or received a hug since I was sixteen goddamn years old, and fuck if it doesn't feel good.

"I know, brother. But that's why you get help. If you can't do it for me, then do it for Ben."

Henry cries in my arms for a long while, and I don't let go. Not until the front door opens and the mood in the room changes dramatically.

"What are you doin' in my house?" Talynn demands, eyeing me up and down and rushing to Henry's side. "Are you okay?"

Henry wipes away his tears with the bottom of his shirt. "I'm fine."

"I just came by to catch up. I'll get gone now," I say and move to the front door. "Think about what I said, Henry."

He nods, and I walk out, shutting the door behind me. My eye catches on a bird figurine in a hanging pot of pansies. I snag it. It's stupid how I keep taking shit from her, but I can't help myself.

I've almost made it to my bike when Talynn stops me.

"What did you say to him?" she hisses.

"That conversation is between him and me." I square my shoulders, feeling a fight coming.

"He was fine when I left. I convinced him to stay."

"By withholdin' money? If you don't get him help, it won't be long 'fore he's pawnin' all your shit to get money for a ticket back to Dallas."

"He wouldn't," she says, but I see the doubt in her beautiful brown eyes. It's hard for me to reconcile this sexy spitfire with the sneaky little girl I used to know. The gap in time where I wasn't part of her life is a black hole I wish I could've been around to see.

"He will. You gotta give him a reason to stay, Tal."

"That's Deputy Davis to you."

I slap on my helmet. "Yeah, okay. If there's nothing else, Deputy Davis, I got chores to do."

She stands on her porch, hands on her hips, and watches me drive away.

CHAPTER 6
TALYNN

Give him a reason to stay.

Colt's words echo through my head, and I wish he was still here in front of me so I could yell at him more. He has no clue how many reasons I've given Henry to stay. He's been around for a couple days, but I've been around my whole life.

Ever since the first time Henry upped and left, I've been giving my brother reasons to not leave me and Daddy. He ignores every single one. I hope this time he'll consider changing his life around, but I'm not holding my breath.

"What did you say to him?" Henry asks when I walk in.

I wipe my brow. "Nothing. Just tellin' him to go away. He has no right comin' into my house."

"We were just talkin', Tal. He didn't mean nothin' by it."

"Yeah, well. He has no business coming anywhere near our family. He's done enough damage." I sit down on the messy couch, part of me dying inside because Henry is treating my living room like he did his bedroom as a teenager.

I won't say anything, though. I don't want to risk him overreacting and leaving.

"Did you stop by the ATM?" Henry asks, changing the subject.

I wince, knowing this was coming. I tried to come up with a believable lie the whole way home but couldn't think of one.

"It was out of service, and the bank was closed when I got there." There. That sounded good.

"I know what you're doing." Henry stands to pace. He has on a short-sleeved shirt today, putting all his track marks, new and old, on full display. His arms are also covered in scabs and bruises, just like his face.

"I'm not doing anythin'."

"You're keeping me prisoner here."

I laugh humorously. "You're not a prisoner. You can leave anytime you want."

"With what money? I'm not asking for a lot. Just

a hundred bucks to get me back to Dallas. I know a guy who was working on getting me a job. I can pay you back."

I'm not an idiot. I know there's no job.

"If it's a job you need, Mr. White is getting on in age and could use some help. He told me so himself. I could tell him you're lookin'."

"I don't want to be in this stupid town, Tal. Don't you get it?"

"Believe it or not, I do. I never thought I'd be able to stay either. But I can still see Ben runnin' through the backfield. And I see Mom at the Get Go, smelling the oranges until she finds the perfect one. How could I not stay here when their memories are here?"

"Exactly. It's the memories I'm trying to escape."

"You need to make peace, Henry. The only other option is to keep tryin' to escape them. And that option will kill you someday."

He storms into the bathroom and slams the door, making the walls shake.

I sigh and dig my cell out of my pocket. Stepping into my backyard, I take a seat at my turquoise bistro set and call my best friend, Sarah.

"Hey, babe. What's up?"

"Henry's home," I say.

She gasps. "Really? Why?"

I spend the next ten minutes catching her up on everything that's happened with Henry and Colton—all of it.

"No shit," she says when I'm done.

"Yeah."

"What an asshole, comin' back here and puttin' your family through this."

"I agree."

"I'm sorry. I don't know what else to say."

"What are you going to do?" she asks.

"Not sure. Right now, I need to focus on gettin' Henry to rehab. He wants me to give him money to get back to Dallas, but I keep puttin' it off."

"If he doesn't want to go, there's no point in sendin' him. You know that, right?" Her tone is cautious because she knows how riled up I get.

"This time is different, Sarah. I'm telling you. He was home alone all day and didn't leave. I can sense he wants to change. He's just. . . waiting for a reason to stay." I repeat Colt's words, realizing how true they are. Everything I've tried in the past hasn't worked; I need to try something else.

"Want me to come over and talk to him?" she asks.

Henry and Sarah have a complicated past. There was a six-month period when Henry did come home to get better. He refused inpatient treatment but enrolled in an outpatient program. He was going to therapy, and we were all convinced the worst was behind us.

Sarah and I had just graduated high school. We were basically glued at the hip for the whole summer before I started classes at the community college, and she went away to attend the University of Texas in Dallas. Henry tagged along on our trips to the creek or town for ice cream, and eventually, they took a liking to each other.

They dated all summer and fell in love. It was weird to have my brother and my best friend together, but Sarah put the smile back on Henry's face, and for that, I was grateful.

But like all good things, the summer ended, and Sarah left, taking Henry's smile with her. He stuck around for a week after that but then took off in the middle of the night, and we didn't hear from him for months. All that progress for nothing.

"No. I don't think that's a good idea. It'll put ideas in his head," I say.

Years after Sarah moved back to Diamond, she admitted that Henry showed up in Dallas. At first, she was happy to see him and took him in since she had an apartment off-campus. But things spiraled quickly.

Henry found a group of friends who liked to party, and he started using again.

He stole from Sarah, lied to her, and one night while high off his ass, he took her car and totaled it. After that, she kicked him out and hasn't seen him since.

"Okay. I understand. But you let me know if you need anything."

"I will. Love you."

"Love you too."

The next morning, I wake up with a pit in my stomach.

He's gone. I just know it.

Jumping out of bed, I run into the living room to find my blankets folded nicely with a note on top. I can guess what it says, something about how sorry he is, but he just can't do it, and he loves me for trying.

I ignore the note for now and immediately go to my kitchen. Getting out the step stool, I climb up and reach for the coffee can hiding behind all my baking supplies.

I sit at my dinette, full of dread. Slowly pulling

the lid off, I'm not surprised to find it empty. He must've found it while I was at work yesterday. My five-thousand-dollar emergency fund is gone.

Propping my elbows on the table, I place my head in my hands, feeling the urge to cry but swallowing it down. This is my fault. I should've moved it, but he was always around, and I didn't want to raise suspicion. Stupid mistake.

I stand and take a calming breath that doesn't work. I should be placing my anger solely on Henry's shoulders, but I'm not. Instead, the red-hot rage burning in my chest is for Colton. Every bad thing that's happened to me since I was twelve is his fault. My current situation included.

I fume as I shower and ready myself for the day. What gives him the right to stroll back into town and fuck with my life again? The man must thrive on my pain. Why else would he keep driving the knife deeper into my heart?

By the time I get in my car, I'm so mad I can't see straight. I start my shift in ten minutes, but instead of driving to the Sheriff's Station, I turn my car in the other direction, toward Diamond Kings Ranch.

Skidding to a stop, I don't turn off the ignition before storming up to his newly repaired door and banging on it. I hear some shuffling inside, then he's standing in front of me in only a pair of tight boxer briefs.

I was right. His broad chest and six-pack abs are chiseled from stone. His pecs are dusted in dark, coarse hair, with a thinner patch starting at his naval and traveling down between a muscled V.

His hair is wild, and his cocoa-brown eyes are bleary as he stares at me in question.

The fact that my body responds to him only makes me angrier. What kind of person is attracted to their brother's killer? A sick one, that's for sure.

"Tal?"

"Deputy Davis," I hiss, and he rolls his eyes.

"Why are you here at this hour, Deputy Davis?"

I start work at five a.m., so I know it's just shy of that time, but I don't feel bad. Don't ranch hands wake up early?

"He left, and it's all your fault," I say.

He sighs and walks away, leaving the door open. I'm not done talking to him, so I follow him inside to find him pulling on a pair of jeans in the doorway to his bedroom but leaving them unbuttoned. He drags his feet to the coffee maker, places a pod inside, then hits the brew button.

"Cup of coffee?" he rasps, his voice still thick with sleep.

"I don't want your coffee. I want you to leave. Don't you see that you're not good for this town?"

"Not good for the town or not good for you?" He trains those serious eyes on me. Did prison make them hard? Because they were full of light and mischief when he was sixteen.

"Both. You're like a cancer, sucking the life out of everyone you're near. Don't you think you've done enough damage?" I croak and could kick myself for showing him any other emotion besides my anger.

He offers me the coffee, and I take it to give my hands something to do other than strangle him. "I don't have cream or sugar or anything."

"I don't want cream or sugar or this coffee. I just want you gone."

"Listen, Ta—" He corrects himself. "Deputy Davis. I'm not causin' trouble. I thought I could talk Henry into getting better. Obviously, I couldn't, so I'm bowing out of that fight. I reckon that means I won't see you again after this visit."

"You realize the Diamond Kings are a motorcycle gang, right? You're practically asking to go back to prison. Somethin' I can't wait to see."

"I don't know what you're talkin' about. We are motorcycle enthusiasts who run this here ranch and do a pretty good job keepin' this precious town you love free of drugs and gangs." He rests a hip on the kitchen counter, crossing his ankles.

"You don't think we know you're runnin' guns?" I smile when his eyes widen a fraction. "We know. We just haven't caught you yet."

I leave out the fact that Daddy has no interest in going after the club. Colt wasn't lying when he said the club does a good job at keeping the filth out of Diamond. And as repayment for their *services*, we're encouraged to leave the club be.

"Like I said, I'm here to tend to the horses and live a quiet life. That's it."

I set the mug on the small dining table and turn to leave. But there's one question that's been bugging me. I shouldn't ask. I should walk out the door and regroup—figure out how to either get him back behind bars or leave town.

"Why did you come back?" I ask with my back to him.

"What?"

"You could've gone anywhere else. Started a new life where no one knows you or what you did. Why did you come back?"

"This is my home. The only place I've ever known. I wouldn't know where else to go."

CHAPTER 7
CROW

My day didn't get better after my rude wake-up call this morning. The wheelbarrow of horse shit tipped over twice, one of our horses, Whisper, had an abscess on her hip and the vet had to be called to drain it, and I lost a wrestling match with some barbed wire, leaving me with gouges all over my arms.

I decide a ride is the only thing that'll turn my mood around, so I saddle Sugar up, and we head out. I keep her at a comfortable clip, chasing the sunset until we reach the top of the hill on the far side of the property. I hop down and leave her to graze as I plop down on the dirt and watch the fiery sky in front of me grow dark while Talynn's question runs through my head.

Why did you come back?

I'm not an idiot. I knew people would have shit to say about it, but when decisions were made about where I'd live when I left prison, I reverted to that sixteen-year-old kid I was when I got locked up. And what does every kid want when they're in a vulnerable position? They want to go home.

I didn't have anything or anyone waiting for me, but this land, this town, and these people were all I knew. I hoped enough time had passed that people might not remember me. The fact that the club nicknamed me Crow only helped cement the idea in my head that I wouldn't be found out. And it was working until Deputy Davis found out about me.

Because I had no ties to the outside, I didn't know the Davis family still lived here. After losing Ben, I thought they'd want to start over somewhere else. I guess that's what they thought I'd do too.

Sugar nuzzles my shoulder, and I stroke her nose. "You know how I stole the seashell soap?" I chuckle. "I stole something else while I was in her house yesterday." Sugar huffs. "Don't give me that. It was just a small bird figurine."

When she showed up this morning, I nearly forgot about the two trinkets sitting on my windowsill. I had to quickly hide them before she barged in and saw. I have no idea how I'd explain that one to her.

Sugar stomps her hoof. She doesn't like the dark, and we're losing light. I mount her, giving her more pats along her neck.

We ride slower on the way back, much to her dismay. Seeing the miles of land around me makes me almost giddy. For so long, *as far as the eye could see* was about six feet to the other side of my cell. Now, my eyes can see plenty far, and I'm free to explore all of it. I can't imagine this feeling ever getting old.

Once Sugar is tucked away for the night, I head to the clubhouse for church. While I was on parole, I stayed behind the scenes of our gun operation. Now that the law isn't breathing down my neck, I'm more involved, and soon, I'll be going on my first run.

Illegal activities should worry me, seeing as I've been on the inside. Instead, having experienced it takes away my fear. I survived, and while I never want to go back, it's not the worst thing that can happen to someone.

I know that for a fact. Because the worst thing that can happen to a person is losing everyone and everything they ever loved.

Walking up the chip aisle, I toss five different kinds in the cart. I didn't have anyone to put money on my account for the commissary in prison, but I ran laundry for twenty-five cents an hour. It was enough for me to buy the occasional ramen and a few hygiene items but nothing more.

Now that I'm out, I can't seem to stop myself from buying snacks. A lot of them aren't nearly as good as I remember. I lived off gummies, toaster pastries, and crackers with squeezy cheese as a teen. Those were the first things I bought when I got a paycheck on the outside, only to learn that as an adult, they're gross.

But things like chips and cookies taste just as good, so I always keep a stock of both. If it weren't for my active job and nightly workouts, I'd have gained twenty pounds by now.

I'm looking at my phone to see what's next on my list when my cart crashes into something. Looking up, I see Mrs. Crawford, the Davis' crotchety neighbor from when I was a kid.

I can't tell you how many times she chased us out

of her backyard with a broom. It didn't stop us from doing it since her backyard was a shortcut home from school, but she nailed us in the head with that broom more than once.

"Excuse me, ma'am," I veer my cart to the side and tip my ball cap down to hide my eyes.

"I know who you are," she says, her tone full of spite.

Anxiety claws at me. Until now, if someone knew who I was, they didn't say shit about it. It made me complacent, so this attack catches me off guard.

I don't acknowledge her, pushing my cart a little faster to get away.

"You killed that sweet boy," she hollers after me. "You and Henry, you were always up to no good. I knew it. The town knew it. But Ben? He was nice and moral."

I freeze, the familiar pain of that day coming back. Ben was all those things, but he was also smart as hell and gentle as a lamb. Henry and I couldn't relate to him at all. We were rough and tumble, always looking for a thrill, no matter the outcome.

The wheels of her cart squeak as they grow closer, but all my self-preservation flies out the window, and my feet stay rooted to the stained linoleum floor.

"I'm talkin' to you," she bites out.

"You okay, Mrs. Crawford?" A man, the store manager, so his name tag says, approaches. "This guy bothering you?"

"Do you know who this is, Stan?" she asks.

He looks me up and down, not missing the Diamond Kings cut I'm wearing.

"No, who is he?"

"He's the one who killed the Sheriff's poor little boy." Mrs. Crawford's tone is laced with venom, and every word she speaks is another punch to my gut.

"Colton Masters?" Stan dips down to see under the bill of my cap. "That you? I thought you were locked up."

"I hear he got out a couple years ago. I complained to the sheriff, but he said his hands are tied."

I guess Talynn wasn't lying about the town not wanting me here.

"I'm gonna ask you to leave. You're causing Mrs. Crawford distress, and that's not good for her weak heart," Stan says.

"Let me check out, and I'll be gone," I mutter.

"That won't be possible. I need you to leave now." He tries to take my cart, but my hands are fisted around the handle and won't let up.

"I have every right to shop here. Let me pay for

my shit, and I'll go." I jerk the cart from his grasp and walk toward the register.

The good boy in me is screaming to let it go and get the hell out of Dodge, but that part of me isn't in charge now—the part of me that's tired of being treated like shit is.

"Cindy, can you call the Sheriff's Office? Tell them we got a disturbance," Stan says.

I get in line, feeling the eyes of every customer in the store on me. The lady in front of me, her cart loaded to the top, moves to the side, no doubt sensing shit is about to go down. I take her spot, tapping my toe as the elderly lady at the register fishes through a stack of coupons.

I tug at my collar, feeling sweat drip down my back.

I can still run. There's time before the sheriff gets here. It doesn't have to happen like this.

Yet, I stay put.

The automatic doors open with a *whoosh,* and without looking, I know it's the authorities. I can only hope Talynn is off duty tonight.

"What's going on, Stan?"

I'm the unluckiest bastard alive because it's Talynn's sweet voice that asks the question. Fuck my life.

"I've asked this gentleman to leave, and he refuses."

My eyes are still trained on the ground so I can't see what's going on, but I imagine Stan's finger-pointing in my direction.

"Of course," she says under her breath, and I listen as footsteps near me. "That true, Colt?"

I tip my head to the side, just enough to catch her gaze. "I'm leavin'. Right after I pay for my groceries."

"He's making everyone here uncomfortable, and we reserve the right to refuse service to anyone. Right now, I'm reserving the right to not serve him."

I'm starting to hate this Stan guy. I don't remember who he is, but he was probably the kid eating his own boogers in the back of the class.

"Looks like you gotta go, Colt. I don't want any trouble, so nothin' else will happen if you decide to walk out those doors. If you don't, I'll have to take you in."

"You're gonna arrest me for existing?" I ask.

"No, I'm going to arrest you for trespassing."

This is bullshit, and she knows it. Or she would if she could bury her hatred for me long enough to be neutral. My guess is that's asking too much.

"Colton," she scolds.

I should give them what they all want, to see me get carted out of here in handcuffs. Then they can all go home and gossip about how Colton Masters is still a bad egg. But that's my pride talking, not my logic.

Shoving the cart away, it crashes into the magazine rack, and I walk out the door, kicking rocks through the parking lot like a toddler throwing a tantrum. I hop up into my truck and slam the door shut. My fists beat on the steering wheel, releasing all my anger and embarrassment from the situation.

All I wanted was some goddamn chips.

A knock on my window startles me, and I see Talynn holding three grocery bags. She backs up so I can open the door.

"Here," she says, thrusting the bags at me.

Peering inside, it's everything that was in my cart. My brows furrow as I take her in.

"It doesn't mean anythin'. I didn't want Stan to have to restock half the snack aisle," she says.

Did she crack a joke? I can't tell.

I pull out my wallet and pull out forty bucks. "Thanks."

"Like I said, it doesn't mean anything." She turns to leave but stops and calls out, "If I were you, I'd shop in the next town over. Stan put you on the trespass list, so if you go back in there, I'll have no choice but to arrest you? And Colt? I'd fuckin' love to put you back behind bars. We all know that's where you belong."

CHAPTER 8
TALYNN

"Are you kiddin' me?" Sarah asks, her jaw dropping.

"Nope." I dump a packet of sugar in my coffee.

It's been a week since I was called to remove Colt from the Get Go, and I still have no clue why I had Nelly ring up Colt's groceries for me. I blame it on the training that taught me to be impartial when I'm on the job. Removing our history from the equation, I saw a defeated man being publicly ridiculed.

I save being a judgmental bitch for my coffee dates with Sarah.

"I can't imagine how hard this is for you."

"I'm so angry, and I have no way to get it all out."

"How's your dad taking everything?" she asks.

"He's not. He's too busy worryin' about me. With

Colton coming back and Henry leaving, he's treatin' me like a ticking time bomb. It pisses me off even more." I watch the swirl of the creamer as I dump the powdery stuff into my coffee.

"I'm sure in a lot of ways, he feels like you're the only family he has left, and he wants to protect you."

"That's not how it feels to me. He's protecting Colton, and as far as Henry goes, he's given up. I just don't understand."

She places her hand on mine from across the table. "He loves Henry. I think he's probably waitin' for him to hit rock bottom."

"Colton found him next to an abandoned building, beat up, with a needle in his arm. How much farther can he fall?"

"I don't know, but I'm sure you'll find out. I just hope it's before he kills himself."

I close my eyes, her words hitting me hard because I know she's right. "I can't lose someone else, Sarah. I can't. And if Henry loses this battle, it'll only make me hate Colton more."

Her green eyes narrow on me. "Henry is responsible for his own life, Tal."

"He was the catalyst," I defend.

"Maybe, but if that's an excuse, why can you hold

down a job, own a house, and be the best plant mom in the world?"

I sigh. "I don't know."

"Exactly. Henry chose to lose the battle with his demons, and honestly, none of us can say with certainty that he wouldn't have turned to drugs anyway. He was constantly in trouble when he was a kid. He broke a record in suspensions. Both him and Colton took their bad-boy image to the extreme."

"I guess."

"I hate to leave you like this, but my lunch is almost up. I need to get back to work." She digs her wallet out of her bag, but I wave her off.

"It's my turn to pay."

"Thank you."

We both stand and collide in a hug that I desperately need. We rock back and forth a few times before parting.

"I love you, Tal."

"Love you too."

She leaves, and I throw some cash on the table to pay for our coffee and pastries. I wave to a few people as I walk out and get in my car. After checking in with dispatch to let them know I'm back from lunch, I pull onto Main Street, ready to get to work.

I'm patrolling when my cell phone rings. It's an

unregistered number, something I only see from telemarketers, but I answer anyway. It's a slow day at work.

"Hello?"

"Tal?" Henry croaks.

My stomach sinks, and the hairs on my arms stand on end.

"What's wrong?" I blurt out.

"I'm sorry. I'm so sorry." He sounds panicked, unnerving me.

"For what? What's going on?" I pull over to the side of the road.

"I fucked up, and I need help."

In the past when he's called to ask for money, he chats me up first, making me believe he called to catch up. This is different. Something's wrong.

"What do you need?"

There's a scuffle, and Henry lets out a pained cry.

"Your brother fucked up, Talynn Davis of Diamond, deputy for the Sheriff's Department who lives on Lilac Ave," a sinister-sounding man says.

"Who is this?"

"Name's Dario."

"Why do you have my brother?"

"He owes me ten grand. I was gonna kill him, but he said he could get that ten grand from you."

"What for?" I ask.

"Your dipshit brother came to me last week asking to resell some of my product but I don't trust my shit with addicts. When he flashed five grand in cash for a deposit, I decided to give him a shot. He was supposed to bring back another five thousand and keep the rest for himself. Wish I could say I was surprised when he didn't deliver." He tsks condescendingly. "My guy found him with no money and no dope."

"I told you, someone stole it," Henry says, his voice shaking.

"Someone stole it because you got your ass so high, you couldn't keep it safe." I hear the distinct sound of a fist connecting with flesh before another wail from Henry.

"Don't hurt him," I plead.

Dario laughs. "Bitch, Imma 'bout to kill this motherfucker unless you can get me my ten Gs. You feel me?"

"You said five. Not ten."

"Consider it a pain and suffering fee."

My mind immediately goes to where I can get that kind of money. Henry stole my emergency cash, obviously using it to buy drugs, and my bank account is at an all-time low after my latest remodeling project.

"How long do I have?" I ask.

"Three days. And for a little incentive, just know that I'll make those three days hurt for this piece of shit."

My vision blurs with unshed tears. I don't have to see the punches and kicks to know what the sounds over the line are, and I startle with each one.

"Stop!" I cry. "I'll do it! I'll get you the money."

"You better. Call me at this number when you have the cash. Oh, and Talynn? The only cop I want to see is you. If I get a whiff of you organizing any more pigs, your brother is dead."

"Okay."

The line goes dead, leaving me a shaky, crying mess. What do I do now? If I tell Daddy, he'll get the cops involved, and they'll kill Henry. I don't doubt it for one second. These aren't dime bag dealers. If they had that much product sitting around, they're at least mid-level players.

Damn it, Henry.

I can sell things. I have a truck that barely gets driven. It's older, but I could probably get five or six grand for it. I don't know how I'll explain that to Daddy, but I can worry about that later.

That leaves me five grand short. I could sell some of my furniture and collector's albums. But that takes longer than three days, and even if I get the money, can I go there by myself? I need backup. Maybe I could talk one of the other deputies into coming along.

I mentally run through my co-workers, ultimately deciding none of them can be trusted with this. They're too loyal to Daddy, and I can't risk that. I need someone who has no issue bending the law.

Shit.

I need Colton.

The rest of my shift flies by as I work through my plan. By the time I get home, I'm still not sure I can come up with that much money, but I can come close. If I have to ask Daddy for a loan and make up some excuse, I will. Daddy comes from family money. Great Granddad and Grandpa were ranchers, and after they both passed, Daddy sold everything since he wasn't interested in ranching. I know he has the money.

I take a quick shower before standing in front of my closet in a towel. What do you wear when you need to ask your brother's murderer to help with a drug deal gone bad? I slap a hand to my forehead. How did I end up here?

Ultimately, I throw on a tank top and a pair of worn jeans, rolling them up past my ankle so I can wear my mid-calf boots with the fringe on the side. As always, my hair is a frizzy mess from the humidity, so I pull it up into a messy high bun. I cried off all my makeup after the call earlier, so I quickly re-apply some mascara and lip gloss. There's no need for more. I'm not trying to impress anyone.

Hopping into my 2001 Toyota Tundra, I head over to the Diamond Kings Ranch. The other two times I've been here, I didn't take the time to get a look at the place because I was beyond heated. But now that I'm here for other reasons, I give it a good, hard look.

There's a big cabin at the way back of the property surrounded by a bunch of smaller cabins, where the guys must all live. The stables are to the side of the living quarters, and if I didn't think the MC was a bunch of low-life degenerates, I'd be impressed with how nice they are. Beyond that is a fenced-off pasture full of beautiful horses.

Stepping out of the truck, I catch a few looks from the MC members, but they must know who I'm here for because none of them approach me. Fear isn't something I submit to, but if I did, I'd be more than a little afraid of them. Each of the men has a dangerous air about them. Their eyes are too dark, their edges too sharp, and their attitudes too bold.

I knock on Colton's door, but there's no answer.

With my hands on my hips, I look around, figuring out which one of the men I should approach. I spot a tall, bearded man with long hair sitting in front of the main building with a beer in his hand and head his way.

"You lost?" he asks.

Glancing at the patch on his leather cut, I see his name is Devil. Huh. Fitting.

I shield my eyes from the sun with a hand. "I'm looking for Col—Crow. I'm looking for Crow."

"He's feeding the horses their dinner." Devil points to the stables.

"Thank you."

"Yep."

The stables match the other log cabin-style buildings, but the inside is gorgeous. Wood and iron cover every surface, and it's the cleanest barn I've ever been in. I look in each stall until I reach one with the gate wide open and a brown Quarter horse tied up inside.

"You see the mess you made? I don't understand why you wait until you get back here to take a shit. You had all day out there in the pasture to do this." Colton scoops a rather large steamy pile of poop and slops it in a wheelbarrow. "All your neighbors wait until after dinner to do this."

I watch as he sets the shovel down and picks up a

brush. He's gentle as he runs it along the horse's back, talking sweet to her as he does.

"Did you have a good day? I didn't. I got to clean up after you fools, then fix the fence y'all destroyed when you got a hair up your ass yesterday. Look at my arms. All tore up thanks to you, and whaddaya give me in return?" The horse nuzzles into his neck, making him smile.

Lord Almighty. Dimples that I forgot he had pop out and the worry lines along his forehead smooth, making him look ten years younger. It's so damn hard to reconcile this man with the one who shot my brother. After twenty years, my mind has conjured him into a cold-blooded murderer, complete with a murderous glare and hate in his heart.

This man doesn't fit into that image. Not at all.

And it's messing with my head.

CHAPTER 9
CROW

A throat clears, and my smile falls, the hard facade I wear returning. Glancing over, I see none other than Talynn Davis, the woman who can't stand me yet keeps making an appearance in my life.

"What do you want?" I ask coldly. I get that she thinks I ruined her life, but there's only so much abuse a man can take.

Her hand goes to her chest. She's taken aback by my greeting. Good.

"I'm sorry to disturb you, but I was hopin' we could talk."

After setting down the brush, I lift the wheelbarrow handles and push past her. "So, talk."

She follows me out, latching the stall shut on her way out. "Henry is in some trouble."

"Seems like he's always in some trouble." I have a long stride, and she struggles to keep up, but I'm not slowing down for her.

"It's serious this time."

We make it to our manure compost bins, where a shovel is waiting for me. "Last time I got involved with Henry, you bit my head off."

"I-I'm sorry about that."

Shoveling the shit into the pile, I ask, "What do you need from me, Talynn?"

"I need your help." Her light brown eyes, that are the color of crystalized sugar, plead with me.

Goddamn, she's beautiful. She's wearing a cropped tank top and low-rise jeans that show off her curvy hips and the slight swell below her belly button. In my nonexistent experience, that's my favorite part of a woman. I can imagine how soft and sensual it must be to run my hand—

My cock thickens, and I shake that thought from my head. I can't think that way. There's not a chance in hell I'll ever experience what this woman has to offer.

I push the shovel back into the manure bin before lifting the wheelbarrow handles back up and returning it to the stable. "What kind of help?"

"This would be a lot easier if I didn't have to chase you around the ranch."

Stopping in my tracks, I turn to her, hands on my hips. "Sorry for not droppin' everythin' I'm doing to talk to the woman who hates my guts and has done everything in her power to make my life hell."

She matches my energy, a scowl forming on her face, and fuck me if it's not adorable. "Are you tryin' to say you don't deserve it?"

"Maybe I do, and maybe I don't. Not for me to judge. But I sure as shit don't have to take it when you're not wearin' a uniform."

She looks to the sky as if she's asking for the Lord's help. "Listen, Colton. This isn't easy for me. Trust me when I say this is the last place on earth I want to be, and you're the last man I want to talk to. If that doesn't tell you how serious this is, I don't know what will."

I blow out a breath. "Fine. We can talk in my cabin."

She silently follows me to my place. I take my boots off and leave them outside, then hold the door open for her, motioning to the sofa.

After her tantrum with my futon, I had to buy something new. I found a sofa at the thrift shop that's ugly as sin, but it was cheap and small—my only two requirements.

She takes notice, running her hand over the emerald-green crushed velvet. Like I said, it's ugly.

"This is new."

"Yeah, some wild banshee with a superiority complex tore up my last one."

She frowns. "I had a warrant."

"You did." I point to my new wall art. "The guys framed it for me."

"That's actually pretty funny." She grins.

"I guess." I sit next to her, stretching my legs out long and leaning back into the cushions. "So, what's up?"

"I got a call earlier." She runs her hands up and down her thighs, and I swear to Christ, I can almost feel what it would be like to be those hands. "When Henry left, he took my emergency cash. He then used that money to buy a whole lot of heroin. He was supposed to sell it and bring back the profits. I'm sure that was his intention, but he ended up using, fell asleep, and the rest of it was stolen."

"Let me guess, the dealer isn't too happy about not gettin' the rest of his money?"

"No." Her eyes water, and her lower lip trembles.

"They beat him up and told me if I didn't bring ten grand, they're gonna kill him."

My arm itches to draw her into me, comfort her, and tell her it'll be okay. Maybe if things were different, I'd have the right to do something like that. Instead, I extend my arm over the back of the sofa. It's as close as I'll ever get to holding her to me.

"Why don't you call your daddy? I'm sure he'd help."

"He would, but he'd do it by the books. He'd alert the local cops and get them involved. The guy said he'd kill Henry if any other cops showed."

"Do you have the money?"

"Not yet. I'm headed to the dealership after I leave here to sell my truck. I think I can get five grand for it. I haven't figured out how to get the rest."

"You got a credit card you can take an advance on?"

She ponders that for a second. "I didn't think about that. I do, but my limit is three thousand."

"So you need two more. Is that why you're here? Because I'm broke." It's a lie. I've been on two runs with the club and walked away five Gs richer.

"I don't want your money. I want your protection."

Something about that makes my ego grow two sizes, but it also confuses the hell out of me.

"You don't trust me," I say.

"I don't."

"Then why do you assume I'll keep you safe?"

"Everyone in my life follows the rules. They'd all try and get Henry back through the proper channels."

"Maybe that's the best solution," I say.

"You didn't hear this man. He was pure evil. I don't doubt for one second he'd kill Henry." She shudders and wraps her arms around herself, which pushes her tits together. My eyes zero in on the cleavage she created.

Noticing where I'm looking, she releases herself and sets her hands on her lap.

I need to get laid. I can't explain why I haven't. It should've been the first thing I did as a free man. But I don't like crowds anymore, thanks to an overcrowded prison, so I can't just go up to the bar like some of the guys do. And everyone local hates me, leaving me at a loss.

I clear my throat and lean over, resting my forearms on my thighs. "So you want me to go to Dallas with you and do what?"

"I think they'll take me more seriously just by you bein' there."

I'm not a small guy, and I know I have a roughened exterior, so I get where she's coming from. But can I do this? I'm not worried about the drug dealer. I know guys like him, and they don't intimidate me. What does worry me are the feelings I have for Talynn. I have no reason in hell to be this attracted to her, but I am. Spending that much time with her and involving myself in her family more is a recipe for disaster.

"I don't know," I say.

"You owe me." I can tell those three words were her backup plan. She was holding them on the tip of her tongue, waiting to throw them at me and knowing I couldn't say no after hearing them.

And I won't. I'd give my life to this family over and over again.

"Fine. When do you want to leave?"

"He gave me three days, but I can't wait that long knowin' they're hurting him. Give me the rest of the day to come up with the money. I'll call in sick to work tomorrow, and we can go." She stands.

"You sure about this?"

"Yes."

She walks out the door without a thank you or even looking back. I follow her to put my boots back on when something occurs to me.

"Hey," I call after her. "How you gonna get home after you sell that truck?"

"I'll walk."

"Gotta be five or six miles from your house."

"I know."

"You want a lift?" I ask.

She shrugs. "If you have nothin' else going on."

"I'm done for the night."

The sun is just beginning to set, but the horses are fed, watered, and locked up safe.

"Okay. Let's go. The dealership closes in an hour."

I grab my keys from the hook just inside my door and walk over to my truck, eyes on Tal. She steps up on her running board and falls behind the steering wheel of her truck.

I'm surprised at her choice of vehicles. The little hippie girl I knew back in the day wanted a baby blue Volkswagen Beetle. Her parents used to say she was born in the wrong era, and they weren't wrong. I remember her twirling in the fields, the sun catching on the natural golden highlights in her hair, while she sang songs by The Beatles.

Henry and I thought she was ridiculous back then. We didn't understand that a free spirit isn't held to social standards the way we were. People labeled us as bad eggs, and we thought that gave us free rein to be shitheads when we were just fulfilling the societal role we were given.

Not Talynn. She always marched to the beat of her own drum, never caring what people thought of her, and I can tell she hasn't changed. Everything about her is a surprise, and it leaves me wanting to sit back and watch her like a movie as she uncovers all her mysteries for me.

As I follow her down the road, it hits me that it's not only my dick that likes Talynn Davis. It's all of me—my heart, my mind, my soul—which means only one thing.

I'm fucked.

CHAPTER 10
TALYNN

That went as well as it could, I think as I pull into the dealership. He gave a hard time, which was to be expected. In the end, I got what I needed from him—protection.

I know I can take care of myself. I'm an excellent shot and have trained with men three times my size to take down opponents, but men like the one holding Henry equate size and attitude with power. I lack in both, so having Colton there will undoubtedly make them think twice about messing with me.

Parking my truck, I look around and gather my personal belongings into a backpack I brought. Colt is waiting for me when I hop down.

"You don't need to come in with me," I say when what I mean is, I don't want to be seen with him. My manners stop me from being that blunt. Not when he's doing me a favor.

"It's all right. I don't mind." He reaches over my shoulder and shuts my truck door. "How are you going to get around without a vehicle?"

"I can walk or take my work car for longer distances."

He holds the door open for me. "Isn't that using an official vehicle for non-official use?"

"Daddy doesn't mind. It's a perk of being a deputy."

"I see."

I approach the girl behind the concierge desk. Her eyes immediately go to the man behind me and widen, though I can't tell why. She's much younger than me, so unless she's heard rumors, she most likely doesn't know who he is.

"Welcome in. How may I help you?" She ignores me, flashing Colt a blinding smile.

Suddenly, it all makes sense. She's attracted to him. I don't fault her for that. Despite my personal feelings toward him, I can't deny his attractiveness. Especially when he looks the way he does today with dusty jeans, dirty boots, a leather cut, and a Stetson on his head. He's a biker cowboy—a lethal combination.

The one thing I can fault her for, though, is

thinking he's the customer just because of the appendage between his legs.

"Is Clark here?" I ask, my tone sharp.

Her smile falls, and she looks at me. "Do you have an appointment?"

"I don't. Please tell him Talynn Davis is here to see him."

Clark and Daddy grew up together. Because of their friendship, I know he'll give me a fair price.

The girl picks up the phone, still making eyes at Colton, who pays her no attention. "Mr. Hanson, you have a Talynn Davis here to see you." There's a pause before she hangs up. "You can go on back. His office is—"

"I know where his office is," I say and head to the right.

Clark is standing in his doorway when we reach him. His attention lands on Colton, and this time, I know why. Clark held Daddy together through the deaths of Ben and then Mom. Daddy has no doubt told him about Colton moving back to town.

"Talynn," he greets, pulling me in for a hug. "How you doin', kid?"

"I'm good." I pull out of the embrace, not looking forward to my next introduction. "This is Colton. Maybe you remember him."

"I do." He glares at him. "What I don't know is why he's here with you."

"I want to sell you my truck, and Colton offered to give me a ride home."

As though a light has been switched off inside him, Colton changes before my eyes. All confidence is gone, and he seems to retreat into himself the way he did when I tossed his place.

"Okay," he drawls. "Well, come on in."

I take a seat in front of Clark's desk while Colt remains in the background, hands tucked into his pockets, looking as small as he can make himself.

"Tell me why you want to sell your truck," Clark says, resting his forearms on his desk.

I was ready for this question and prepared a lie.

"I have another remodel project in mind and could use the cash. Since my truck just sits in the driveway collecting dust, I thought it'd be the smartest way to get my project done without takin' out a loan."

"You always were a smart girl. Okay, I'll have one of my guys take a look, and we'll see what we can offer. You have a number in mind?"

"It Blue Books for seven, so I think six is fair," I say confidently.

Clark stands and points a finger at me, grinning. "See? Smart girl. Be back in a minute."

An hour and a whole lot of paperwork later, I have a check for six grand.

"Thanks, Clark. I appreciate it," I say, giving him a goodbye hug.

"No problem. You kept that truck in mint condition, so we'll have no problem selling it."

"I have one more favor to ask of you."

"What's that?"

"I need you to not tell my dad. He won't understand my need to do this on my own and will be mad I didn't ask him for the money."

"Always so independent." He gives me a warm smile. "My lips are sealed."

I don't know if I can trust him or not, but it's too late now. I can only hope he waits until after tomorrow if he does tell him. It's not a secret I can keep forever; I just need it kept until I get Henry home safe.

This better be the rock bottom Sarah was talking about because I can't do this again.

"Guess I'm driving tomorrow?" Colton asks as we walk to his truck.

"Will this thing make it?" I pat the hood.

"She's solid. I'd rather take my bike, but I'm assumin' you want to bring Henry home?"

"Yes. Though I doubt he'll want to." I climb into

the truck.

"How are you going to get the rest of the cash? You're running out of time if you want to get this done by tomorrow." He starts his rust-bucket of a truck.

"Can you run me to the bank?" I hate asking him for more favors, but he's right. It's dark out and walking will take too long.

"Sure, but can we get some dinner first. I'm fuckin' starvin'."

"Dinner?" I ask dumbly.

"Yeah. The meal you eat when it's nighttime?"

"Oh. Where do you want to eat?" The thought of anyone around town seeing us share a meal makes my skin crawl and will definitely get back to Daddy. But I can't say that, not when he's helping me out.

"The diner?"

I chew on the inside of my mouth. "Let's run to the bank real quick and then go back to my house. I can whip us up some omelets."

He side-eyes me. "Don't want to be seen with me, huh?"

"It's not that." I have nothing else to add because I don't have a believable excuse.

He nods and turns into the bank parking lot. I get out and withdraw the maximum amount on my credit card. I'm still a grand short, but I'll figure that out when I'm away from Colton and can think clearly.

"Okay, I got it," I say, climbing back into the truck.

"How much are you short?" he asks.

"A thousand."

"I can cover it."

"You don't have to do that."

He turns to face me, draping his arm over the steering wheel. "You don't know me well, so let me fill you in. I don't do anything I don't want to do. Not anymore. So if I offer somethin', it's 'cause I want to."

I stare at him for a long moment, noting the hard set of his jaw and the intensity in his eyes. This man is an enigma to me, as is this bond we share. There's no reason I should be comfortable around him or okay with him helping me, but here I am.

Maybe it's because I grew up with him, and that familiarity was imprinted on my soul? Or maybe I'm using him however it pleases me because I truly feel like he deserves to be at my service after what happened.

God, I hope that's not what this is because it would speak more about me than him, and no one wants to admit they have a nasty side to them. Whatever my reasons, the only thing that's important right now is getting Henry back. After that, I can go my way, and he can go his. I'll thank him for his help but leave him alone and not cause any more drama for him. As long as he stays on the right side of the law.

"Oh. Okay. Well, thank you. I'll pay you back."

"If I said I'd loan you the money, I'd expect repayment. But that's not what I said."

"Regardless, I don't want to feel like I owe you anything, so I will pay you back."

Turning away from me, he wordlessly drives me home. It's unnerving, and I don't know whether it's because he's upset about me not wanting to go to the diner with him or for some other reason. I get my answer when he doesn't turn the truck off in my driveway.

"Aren't you comin' in for dinner?" I ask.

"No, Tal. I'm good. I have a bunch of snacks at home, remember?"

Guilt washes over me for a brief second before indignation pushes it away. "You can't expect me to want to be seen around town with you after what happened."

"Nope. I can't."

Is he being genuine or flippant? I can't tell; he's so hard to read.

"You have to understand where I'm comin' from."

"I do." He stares out the windshield.

"Listen, I appreciate what you're doing, but it doesn't change anything. You have no idea what you put us through after that day."

His jaw ticks.

"What? I can tell you have somethin' to say, so say it."

"Good night, Talynn," he says.

"Fine. Whatever." I slam the door shut and stomp my way to the door. It's childish, but he brings it out in me.

I'm digging my keys from my bag when I hear him call out, "Did you ever stop to think you didn't see what you think you saw?"

I glance over at where he's standing just outside the truck, confused by his meaning. "What?"

"That day. You weren't there when it went down. How can you be so sure about what happened?"

Flashes of memories come back to me. The gunshot, Ben on the ground, Colton holding the gun, Henry devastated. There's only one obvious conclusion. Right?

"What are you trying to say?"

He stares at the stars for a long minute before answering. "Nothin'. Good night."

I can only deal with one thing at a time, and deciphering his cryptic message will have to wait until tomorrow.

"Thanks for today," I say and pull my keys out.

I don't miss how he waits until I'm inside to pull away.

CHAPTER 11
CROW

Talynn walks out of her house looking like she's about to commit a heist with her black cargo pants, a black T-shirt, and black combat boots. All the resentment I'm feeling for her slips, and I have to cover my smile as she walks toward me.

She was probably going for tough, but to me, it's adorable.

Tal said she needed some time to cash the check from the dealership and run a few errands, so it's afternoon by the time I pick her up. This was fine because it meant I could get my morning chores in before we left. I hate pawning shit off on the other guys.

"Hi," she says, not making eye contact. It's not a

good sign as to how today is going to go, but what can I expect after how we left things last night.

"Hey."

She sticks her backpack on the floor between her legs, buckles her seatbelt, and folds her arms. Instead of feeding into her tantrum, I crank the radio and take off toward the highway. It's going to be a quiet, boring ride. Not more than two minutes later, she turns the music down.

"Don't like classic rock?" I ask.

"I don't like loud music. It gives me a headache."

"You can change the station if you want," I offer, trying to keep the damn peace because, at this rate, we'll be screaming at each other the whole way.

"I'd rather just have silence."

Except I'm not good with silence. I didn't get one moment of it for twenty years, and now it makes me antsy. Even in the cabin, I keep the TV on whether I'm watching it or not.

"One of our mares had her foal last night, and I'm wiped, so unless you want me crashin' us into the ditch, you better talk to me or let me listen to the radio."

"What do you want to talk about?" she asks, but her gaze is out the window.

"I don't care."

She flips like a light switch and rotates her body to face me. "All right. Why were you such a dick to me last night?"

Okay, then. Screaming match, it is.

"I wasn't bein' a dick. I declined your offer to make me dinner because you clearly don't think much of my company. That's all."

"How can you not understand that being seen around town with the man who murdered my brother is a poor decision?"

I fucking hate the way she throws that around when she doesn't know shit about what she's saying. She has no clue what happened out there that day because she wasn't really there. Yet that detail doesn't seem to mean fuck all to anyone.

I could lay it out for her and watch as her world is turned upside down, but it's not my story to tell, and I've spent too long being quiet about it to speak up now.

"Knowin' something ain't a good choice and feelin' shitty about it are two different topics, Tal."

"That's fine, but you don't need to make me feel bad about it."

"I never said one goddamn word about it. That was your own conscience speakin' to you."

She chews on the inside of her mouth as she

thinks that over. Pushing back into the seat and refolding her arms, she grumbles, "Whatever."

I pull off to the side of the highway, needing to find a resolution for the sake of my sanity.

"What are you doing?" she asks.

"Listen here. You can hate me with every fiber of your being, and I'm okay with that. I'm okay with you goin' back to makin' my life a living hell. I don't give a shit. But what we're walkin' into once we hit Dallas is gonna require you and me to be on the same page." I motion between us. "I know men like this guy who're holding your brother. Hell, I shared a cell with a few of them, and I'm tellin' you right now, they will smell any bit of weakness and exploit it. So, if you can't get over yourself for one day, tell me now, and I'll take us both home."

The tension in her arms relaxes, and her hands fall to her lap. "You're right. I'm sorry."

"Thank you." I pull back onto the highway, and she turns the radio up enough to be background music. "What was prison like?"

I blow out a breath. There's a lot I'd never tell her. All the dehumanizing and traumatic shit doesn't ever need to be spoken aloud, mostly because I can't think about it, let alone talk about it.

"Lonely."

"You're in there with thousands of other men," she says dumbly.

"Yeah, but"—I push my fingers through my hair, trying to think of how best to describe it—"everyone in there is trying to get more than they're given. Most would turn their backs on their own brothers to earn the trust of someone higher in the social hierarchy or earn stuff like food or access to a cellphone. I saw it early on and chose to mostly stick to myself."

"Makes sense."

"It was also tiring. Every minute of your day is accounted for, and there are no luxuries."

"Duh, you're in prison."

I scoff. "When I say luxuries, I don't mean spa days and brunch. I mean basic things, like heat or air conditionin'. In the winter, it got so cold at night that I'd wake up every few hours to flex and extend my toes and fingers because they literally felt like they'd fall off. Your bed is metal, the mattress pad is an inch thick, and the one blanket and sheet you're given are threadbare."

"Let's talk about something else." She chews on the inside of her mouth.

Either she's thinking she's glad I went through that or maybe she's feeling a touch of guilt. I don't know and I don't ask.

"Okay. How about you tell me what you've been up to the last twenty years."

"Not much more than you can guess on your own. Went to college, followed by law enforcement academy, then got a job workin' for my daddy."

"You never left Diamond?" I ask.

"No. Never had a desire to. Plus, I couldn't leave my dad alone. What about y—" She clamps her mouth shut, realizing she already knows the answer. "Stupid question."

"Not really. Just because I was locked up doesn't mean I didn't do things."

"Like what?"

"I got my GED and then got a scholarship to get my bachelor's."

"You have a college degree?" she asks, shock evident in her tone.

"I do. Not that I'll ever do anything with it. I did it to be productive, you know?"

"That was smart."

After that, we're both quiet, and the Eagles sing about lying eyes to fill the silence. My thoughts wander, wondering what's going on in her head.

It must've been hard for her to come to me for help. In her eyes, I destroyed her life. I ruined everything good she had.

Guess it makes sense, though. What better way to deal with a criminal than with another criminal? Thinking about it that way makes me feel like shit. I don't want to be that person to her. I'd much rather her come to me because I'm her man, and that's what a man does. Fucking sucks it'll never be that way.

"Do you remember the pool parties my family used to have?" she asks, the memories bringing a beautiful smile to her face.

She's changed so much, turned into this beautiful woman with a hard edge that wouldn't be there if Ben hadn't died. But sometimes, like right now, I see that golden glow she had when she was a girl.

"Yeah, I remember."

"Did you know I had a crush on you?"

I scratch my chin, those words taking me back to a time that feels like yesterday and a million years ago at the same time. Her brothers gave me so much shit over their kid sister crushing on me. I wasn't flattered. Matter of fact, it was downright embarrassing. But seeing how she grew up and wanting more than anything for her to look at me like that again, I'm flattered as fuck.

"I had an inkling," I say.

"I loved watching you pull off your shirt." Her

cheeks pink up, and fuck if it's not the sexiest color on her.

"I was scrawny as hell."

"You had some muscles." She reaches over and squeezes my bicep. "I mean, you didn't have all this back then."

Swear to Christ that one small touch has my cock standing at attention. Probably best I'll never get her under me. I'd come the second I got inside her, no doubt about that.

"One good thing about prison, I guess. Lots of time to work out."

Her cheeky smile drops, and once again, the weight of our history is back on her shoulders. I fucking hate that no matter what we talk about, it'll always lead us back to this place where I'm the villain in her story.

We don't try for conversation after that, which is fine by me. I seem to dig my hole deeper and deeper with every topic.

We're about fifty miles outside of Dallas when the engine sputters something ugly, and I'm forced to pull off on the side of the freeway.

"What's going on?" Talynn asks.

"Don't know yet," I say. I have a good idea of

what it is, and if I'm right, this is gonna get messy. "Stay here while I look. It's not safe to be out there."

"Okay."

The wind whips at me from the cars flying by as I walk around to the front of the truck. Popping the hood, I see I was right. Fuck. This isn't gonna go over well.

"Well?" she asks as I get back into the truck.

"You don't happen to have AAA, do you?"

"What's wrong with it?"

"Carburator. Nothin' I can fix without parts or tools. It'll need to be towed." I wince, knowing she's gonna lose it.

"No," she draws out. "Really?"

"Yep."

"I do have AAA. Let me call."

Three hours later, we're sitting in a repair shop, waiting for the bad news. They wouldn't tow us to Dallas, so they dropped us off in some small town I'm not sure has a name. From what I can tell, they have a gas station that doubles as a repair shop, a grocery store the size of a shed, and a motel that doesn't look like it's had a visitor since 1942.

I'll give Talynn credit; she's holding up good. She probably thinks this'll be an easy fix, and we can be back on the road soon. I'm too chicken shit to tell her that's not gonna be the case.

Fred, the only employee in this place, walks into the dingy, smelly waiting room, wiping grease from his hands with a rag that's not much cleaner. Tal and I stand to meet him.

"Well, it's like you thought. You need a new fuel pump," he says.

"You don't happen to have one lyin' around?" I ask.

"Nope, and it's too late to make a run for one. Better you two shack up for the night, and I'll head to Dallas tomorrow morning, get you back on the road by ten, I reckon."

"What? Tomorrow? No. We need to be in Dallas today," Talynn says.

"Sorry, hon. Not gonna happen."

She turns to me and whispers, "I can't leave him for another night."

"You have any rentals or a taxi service of some kind?" I ask Fred.

"No, sir. To be honest, we don't see many people around here. Lou and his wife run the motel across the way. He'll get you set up."

I hold out a hand, and Fred shakes it. "Appreciate it."

"Colt," Talynn scolds as we walk outside.

"There's nothin' I can do. I'm outta options."

Her hands go to the side of her head. "I can't believe this. You said the truck was solid."

"It was," I say. "Until it wasn't."

"This isn't funny. Henry is probably gettin' the crap beat out of him right now. The longer we wait, the worse shape he'll be in."

"I know. Trust me, this isn't ideal, but I don't know what else to do."

"I knew I shouldn't have trusted you," she spits out, and it might be the worst thing she's ever said to me.

I want to argue and remind her how I couldn't have predicted this happening, but it's a waste of time. If she's keeping tally, this is just another strike against me.

CHAPTER 12
TALYNN

I stare at the motel that looks like it could've been a set for an old Western. The one-story, tan stucco building has five rooms, judging by the brown-painted numbered doors. The windows attached to each room are so caked in dirt I doubt you could see through them.

We enter the main door and walk into a room no bigger than a closet. No one sits behind the desk, but there's a bell to push, and I slam my finger down on it. It barely makes a sound. Of course not.

I'm angry and worried, which has me feeling out of control. Since it's Colt's truck and he's the only one around, I know I'm taking it out on him. In the back of my mind, I realize it's not his fault, but damn it, nothing is ever okay when he's around.

"Hello? Anyone here?" Colt bellows in his rich baritone.

There's a hallway behind the counter that I'm assuming leads to the owner's home. Sounds come from back there, and a minute later, an elderly woman with deep wrinkles and thinning gray hair appears.

"Sorry, I don't move as fast as I used to," she says, moving to the desk. "How can I help you?"

"We're lookin' for rooms for the night. Do you have any available?" Colt asks.

"You can imagine we don't get visitors very often." She opens a paper ledger because, of course, she doesn't have a computer. "I've rented out most of my rooms for storage, but I do have one that I keep open."

"We need two," I say.

She peers at me through cloudy blue eyes. "I'm sorry. I only have the one."

"We'll take it." Colt digs his wallet out.

"I'm not sharin' a room with you," I hiss.

"Don't have a choice." He directs his attention to the woman. "How much?"

"Twenty-nine dollars a night."

He removes cash from his wallet and hands it over. "Here you go."

"Okay." She opens a drawer and produces a key. "It's room five. The one on the end."

"Thank you." Colt takes the key and then takes my hand, pulling me outside.

I ignore how good his larger hand feels wrapped around mine and jerk it from his hold the second we step outside.

"There must be another choice. Another town close by. Something."

"This is it, princess. You're lookin' at it." He turns in a circle, his arms outstretched to prove his point. There's nothing here but the gas station that doubles as a car repair station, an RV park that looks mostly inhabited, and this motel.

I snag the key from his hand and stomp to room five. I have zero expectations, but somehow, I'm still disappointed at what I find when I open the door.

There's a small wooden table and two matching chairs in front of the window, a credenza with a TV to the left, and an attached bathroom. Everything is old, covered in dust, and probably crawling with bugs. But what my mind focuses on is the singular double bed along the wall to the right.

"There's only one bed," I deadpan.

"It's fine. I'll sleep on the floor." Colt brushes past me, heading to the check out the bathroom.

I follow. The shower has a dingy curtain, there are rust stains in the sink, and the toilet bowl water is brown.

"I can't believe this."

"I've seen worse," Colt says.

"Yeah, I get it. You were in prison." I leave the bathroom and go to the bed, lifting the mattress to check for bed bugs. Thankfully, there are none that I can see.

"I'm real fuckin' sorry, Tal. This put you in a bad place, and I feel responsible." Colt stands by the door, his hands tucked into his pockets, looking defeated.

"Yeah, I know." I take a seat on the bed, waving away the dust that flies up.

"I'm gonna go get us somethin' to eat from the gas station before they close." He opens the door. "Any requests?"

"I'm not hungry."

"Okay," he says and closes the door behind him.

Alone, I don't feel the pressure to keep myself together, and tears fill my eyes. I let out a choked sob, and despite how disgusting this bed is, I lie down and curl into a ball. What's Henry being subjected to now? Are they beating him? Giving him food and water? Will he be alive by the time we get there?

I have a bad feeling about this entire situation.

Bringing Colt into this was a bad choice. I should've done the right thing and had Daddy take care of it. I'm a deputy for Chrissakes, and instead of relying on the law that I'm sworn to uphold, I asked Colt for help.

Timing Colt's trip to the gas station in my head, I allow myself to wallow for as long as possible, then pull it together and lock myself in the bathroom. I can't let him see me like this, weak and pathetic. For Henry's sake, I need to be strong and fearless.

Staring at my reflection, I remind myself it's just one more day. After tomorrow, things will be better. Henry will get the help he needs, and life can go back to normal. I'll pretend Colt doesn't exist and focus on what's important. My family.

Once the last of my pity party has left me, I step back into the room. Colt's back with two plastic bags on the table.

"What'd you find?" I ask.

"Were you crying?" Colt's penetrating gaze assesses me.

I place a hand on my forehead. "No, just hot. Does this place have air conditioning?"

"You're lyin', but let me see if this unit works." He fiddles with the controls on the window unit. When nothing happens, he crouches down to make sure it's plugged in. It is. He bangs on the unit three times, and surprisingly, it kicks on. "Ah-ha."

"Thank God." A breeze of cool air blows over me from where I sit on the bed.

"Didn't find a whole lot." Colt pulls out a couple bottles of water, some bags of chips, a protein bar, candy bars, and a bag of Skittles. Does he remember they're my favorite? Or is it by chance? I don't ask. Switching to the second bag, he pulls out at least fifteen mini liquor bottles.

"Planning on gettin' drunk?" I ask.

"Nothin' better to do. Figured a couple drinks won't hurt to pass the time." He tosses me one, and I catch it. It's one of my worst enemies, tequila. Of all the liquors, this one lowers my inhibitions the most. I throw it back to him.

"No, thanks."

"You gotta better plan?" He produces a bottle of orange juice. "In prison, we used to make this wine from fruit we'd smuggle off our dinner trays. It tasted like ass, but it got the job done."

"I've heard of toilet wine."

"Pretty gross when you say it like that." He gives me a sheepish smile as he opens a plastic cup next to the ice bucket on the credenza. He pours it half full of orange juice before dumping in a mini bottle of tequila. Repeating the process, he brings both cups over to the bed and sits on the opposite side as me. "Cheers."

I stare at the proffered cup, deciding if drinking is the best thing to do right now. It's early evening, and it's been a horrible day, yet I know I couldn't sleep, and I doubt the TV works.

"Cheers." Taking the cup, I gulp the drink down in one go.

"Really goin' all in, huh?" He smirks with his lower lip perched on the edge of the cup, then he tips it back. I watch as his Adam's apple bobs with each swallow.

My mind and body are constantly at war when I'm near Colton. For a man who took away two of the most precious people in my life—whether indirectly or directly—I can't help but have a fierce attraction to him.

It causes me guilt and shame that even the men I dated in college didn't remotely compare to Colton, which weighs heavy on my conscience and contributes to my resentment toward him.

"Like you said, we got nothin' better to do," I say, scooting so my back is against the wooden headboard.

"Ready for another?" he asks.

"Sure."

He jumps up and repeats the process, pouring the last of the orange juice into the cups. "Gonna have to shoot straight next time."

"I won't be tasting anything by then."

This time when he sits on the bed, he mimics my position. Our shoulders touch as he offers my cup to me. We drink them down together, after which he takes my cup, stacks it with his, and sets them on the nightstand.

"Hate to bring it up, but did you call the asshole who has Henry?"

"No. I figured I'd wait until we were in Dallas."

"After all this"—he circles a finger around the room—"I'm glad you didn't."

"Me too."

"This'll all be over tomorrow, okay?" His tone is definitive. "Swear to God, Tal. I'll make sure of it."

"How can you be so sure?" I ask.

"You know why I joined the Diamond Kings?"

"Because they hire convicts?" I assume.

"That's why I got a job at the ranch. That's not why I joined up."

"You are a motorcycle enthusiast?" I guess. The alcohol is kicking in and loosening my tongue.

"You want to keep guessing, or can I tell you?"

"Tell me."

"They protect everythin' they stand for. Now I need you to tuck away your deputy ears for a minute. Can you do that?"

I nod.

"In our world, there are no laws except the ones we make for ourselves." He cracks his knuckles like he's readying for a fight. "And the biggest one is to protect the club, our brothers, and the people we love. And that means we will do anythin', even if it means breaking laws, to keep our people safe."

"You love Henry?"

"I love your whole family." His words are barely a whisper. "Always have. And I'll protect any one of you with my life. That's somethin' this asshole keepin' Henry can't say. He has no morals, so keepin' himself alive will always be priority one. I guarantee that prick'll run to save his own skin."

I want to ask about Ben. How much could he love him if he shot him? Even if it was an accident, something I think I believe more and more these days. I wish I knew exactly what happened, but I'm too scared to go there. Maybe after this is all over, I can bring it up, but it'd be too much to know now.

"I'm glad I came to you then," I say.

"Me too. And if things get to be too much, I can

have at least ten guys here in a few hours. My brothers have my back, no matter what."

"I can tell that's important to you."

"Hell yeah, it is. I guess that's what attracted me the most to the club. No one had my back when I was younger. No one. Seein' how the guys would go to war for each other, no questions asked, was appealing. The day I patched in is the proudest moment of my life." His chest puffs in satisfaction at the mere mention of the club.

"I haven't had a lot of experience with the club. Y'all seem to keep to yourselves mostly. Other than the occasional bar fight."

"That's because we self-govern. No need for the police." He chuckles and then jumps off the bed. "Ready for another shot?"

"Sure. And pass me a bag of chips." My head is comfortably numb, blocking out all the bad stuff. I'm thankful for the reprieve, and since we're getting along right now, I might as well keep going.

"I knew you'd want snacks." He sits down to remove his boots. When he stands, he pushes off his cut. It's the first time I've seen him without it. His shirt stretches tight along his defined chest and broad shoulders. He's definitely not the sixteen-year-old boy I remember.

Bringing over a bag of nacho cheese corn chips and two more mini bottles of tequila, he reclaims his place on the bed. Not only do our shoulders touch, but now our legs do too. I should move mine, create space between us, but I don't.

"Thanks," I say, setting the chips aside while I unscrew the lid of the cheap tequila. It burns going down, giving me an instant high. This will be my last one. Any more, and I know I'll embarrass myself.

"Tell me about college." His tone is light and conversational, without the usual seriousness he carries.

"What do you want to know?"

"Did you have boyfriends?"

So we're going there. Maybe one more shot wouldn't hurt.

CHAPTER 13
CROW

I shouldn't be asking her about boyfriends. It's none of my business. But ever since she charged into my cabin in that uniform and tight bun, her breasts pulling at the buttons holding it closed, it's something I wonder about.

That's a lie. My thoughts are dirtier.

What I wanna know is how many assholes she's let between her legs, and if there's anyone who treated her badly that I need to teach a lesson to.

"I had boyfriends, yes."

"Couldn't have been very good ones," I mutter.

"Why do you say that?" She peers over at me, her light brown eyes shiny from the liquor.

"Because you dumped them."

If I had a woman like Talynn, there's no way in

hell I'd give her up. I'd fight to the death for her. Do whatever it took to keep that sassy mouth, pretty eyes, and banging body in my life.

"How do you know I broke up with them? Maybe they dumped me."

I shake my head. "No way."

"How can you be so sure?"

"Because men don't let a woman like you go," I say with all the authority in the world.

"Well, you're wrong. I've had two serious relationships, and both times I was dumped." Her expression sours like she's still bitter about it. "Apparently, men don't like women with strong opinions who don't need a man to change their tire or fix a leaky sink."

"That's not a man, Bug."

Her eyes go soft, and her shoulders relax. "You remember the nickname?"

"I remember."

I used to call her Bug because she was so annoying. Henry and I couldn't do shit without her following us, thinking we didn't know she was there, like a pestering bug.

"I thought I was so sneaky." She grins.

"You were not." I smile back at her.

Her whole body turns to face me, her legs crossed.

"What about you? Have you dated since you've been out?"

I exhale audibly. "That requires another drink. Want one?"

"Sure, but only one more. I don't want to feel terrible tomorrow."

I grab two more bottles of tequila and hand one over. We click the little glass necks together and chug. I haven't drunk more than a couple beers since my parole ended, so I'm definitely feeling a nice buzz.

I'm glad I chose to grab the alcohol at the gas station. Things have been tense, and we needed to let loose, even if only for a few hours. I wasn't certain Talynn would participate, but I'm happy she is because this woman was wound so tight, I was worried she'd combust.

"So?" she asks expectantly.

I debate how much truth to give her. I'm embarrassed about my lack of experience, but with the question in front of me, I'm mad I haven't rectified the situation yet.

"No. I haven't dated."

"Why not?"

"Been busy. And since everyone in Diamond hates my guts, I'd have to go to the next town over to meet anyone."

"Wait. Does that mean you're a *virgin*?" She whispers that last word like it's a curse.

Nervous laughter bubbles out of me. I debate lying to her. She'd never know the difference, but I don't want more lies to come between us, so I shoot straight.

"Yup."

"How?" she asks, bewildered.

"How am I still a virgin? Well, I went to prison at sixteen and wasn't released from parole until, what? Two weeks ago? Since then, I found out everyone in Diamond hates me, and I'm too busy to leave town to find someone to fuck."

"Oh. Right."

"I'm not proud of it," I say.

She cackles, then quickly slaps a hand over her mouth.

"You're mockin' me after I admit my most embarrassing secret," I accuse.

"I'm sorry. I'm not poking fun, I swear."

"Then why are you laughing?"

"It's funny that a guy who looks like you is still a virgin. I mean, come on." She motions up and down my body. "You're every woman's wet dream."

"Women don't have wet dreams."

Her spine straightens, and her hands fall into her lap. "Uh, yeah, they do."

Feeling brave from the liquor, I ask, "Who gives you wet dreams?"

She blushes, the beautiful pink spreading over her cheeks, down her neck, and across the small amount of cleavage shown across her chest.

"None of your business," she says.

I smile and decide to let it go. I like this playful banter we have going on. She's treating me like an actual human and not the monster from her nightmares. I wish it was always like this.

"Tell me about all those plants I saw in your house. It looks like your own secret garden in there," I say, changing the subject.

She gets excited about this topic and tells me the names of all her plants and their various personalities. I listen, enjoying how animated she gets when talking about each one.

We talk and laugh for what feels like hours. I even convince her to take two more shots, making her giggly and unusually pleasant. It's the most fun I've had in ages, and by the end of the night, I'm glad my truck broke down because it gave me this memory.

"I think it's time for sleep," she says, yawning and stretching her arms over her head. I catch a sliver of skin where her flat abs meet the rounded curve of her lower belly. My cock thickens painfully. I try to talk myself down and think of anything besides how it would feel to touch her there, but it doesn't work.

"Yeah, probably best." I turn away from her as I stand up and adjust myself so my erection isn't obvious.

"You don't have to sleep on the floor."

"I don't mind." Actually, I'd prefer it. Being that close to her right now would be torture.

I open each drawer in the credenza but don't find any extra blankets. The closet is empty too. Shit.

"No extra bedding?"

"No. I can call and ask if some can be delivered."

"She won't answer. It's late. I don't think you have a choice."

"Are you sure? I don't want to make you uncomfortable."

"It's just sleep. It's fine." She walks into the bathroom, closing the door.

Stripping down to my boxer briefs, I climb in before she sees my hard-on and changes her mind. I should take a shower to rub one out and take the edge off, but I'm tired after a rough day. Add in the tequila, and sleep is sounding good.

Minutes later, she exits the bathroom. I'm facing

away from her, but I peer over my shoulder to see her with her back to me as she lowers her cargo pants to the floor. The top of a black thong appears, then narrows to a strip, and the fabric gets lost between her round cheeks.

Fuck me. If I thought I was hard before, I'm granite now, pre-cum seeping onto my boxers.

Before she catches me, I turn back around and bite my lip so hard that I taste blood. I'd give anything, do anything to be with this woman. Hell, I'd move fuckin' mountains just to get a taste. Knowing it'll never happen is a dagger to the heart. And my dick.

She flips off the light and climbs in, keeping her distance. Thank God. One touch from her right now, and I'd come in my underwear. Since I don't have a spare, I'd have to freeball it tomorrow.

"Can I ask you a question?" Her voice is barely a whisper.

Hesitantly, I roll over. "Sure."

"Do you miss him?" she asks.

We didn't bother shutting the curtains since the window is caked in dirt, so the light from the streetlamp illuminates her just enough to see her down-turned eyes.

"Henry?"

"No. Ben."

My chin drops to my chest. I don't like to think about this, and going down this road will only lead to more pain she'll undoubtedly thrust upon me. But if I can't give her all the answers, I can give her this.

"So much it hurts."

I watch a lone tear spill from her eye and soak into the lumpy pillow. "Me too."

"I'm so fuckin' sorry, Tal. You have no idea."

She sniffles. "That's the first time you said that."

"Might be the first time sayin' it out loud to you, but I think it. Every minute of every day, it crosses my mind at least once." That's the God honest truth.

"I believe you."

There have never been three more powerful words spoken to me. The heavy weight I've been carrying doesn't lift from my chest, but it grows considerably lighter, and for the first time in twenty years, I can breathe. Then something that's never happened to me before—not when I was a scared sixteen-year-old being taken away in handcuffs, not when my parents visited me in juvie and said their goodbyes, and not when I was eighteen and transferred to prison—happens.

I cry.

"Thanks," I say. My voice chokes up, and tears

stream from my eyes like a baby. Rolling onto my back, I bat at them angrily. How have I managed to keep all this suppressed for so fucking long only to have it all come out with Talynn's words?

She scoots closer, lifting up on her elbows. "It's okay, Colt. I didn't mean to make you emotional."

"It's fine." I cover my face with my hands, embarrassed.

"Don't do that." She pulls them away one at a time. "Ever since I came storming into your cabin, this is what I was hoping to see. Any kind of emotion that would tell me what kind of man you've become. But each time I saw you, all you gave me was self-loathing."

"That's not what I feel. I don't pity myself. It's guilt," I admit.

She creeps even closer, placing a hand on my bare chest. "I forgive you."

I freeze because I was wrong. Those words are a million times more impactful than her earlier ones. "I don't deserve anyone's forgiveness."

"I didn't say it for you. I said it for me. I need to let go of the resentment I have for you. It's not good for me."

I nod, thankful the stupid tears have quit. "I get that."

"But you should be proud of the man you turned into. No matter how poorly I treated you, you were there for me and Henry. After everything you've been through, I think that's commendable."

"Thank you."

"This is gonna sound way out of left field, but I'm drunk, and the last twenty-four hours have been exhausting. Would you hold me, please?"

"Uh, yeah. Sure."

I stay still, waiting for her to decide how this should work, willing my body to not betray me. This isn't sexual. It's a vulnerable woman needing support.

She rolls away from me and backs up until her ass hits my thigh. Lifting her head, she says, "This is where the holdin' me part comes in."

"Right." Flipping to my side, I snake an arm under her head. Do I put my other arm around her? Or is that too much? I have no fucking clue.

My questions are answered when she reaches back, grips my hand in hers, and tugs my arm over her middle. She settles my palm along her stomach, and not the flat part, the soft part on her lower belly—the part I've jerked off to more than once.

It's even better than I imagined, but I don't give myself time to think about it because her bare ass is nestled against my pelvis, and I doubt she wants that kind of comfort.

"This feels nice. Thank you."

"Anything for you, Tal, and I mean that."

"I know you do." She yawns, wiggling deeper into the mattress, and I swear to fuck, she better knock that shit off. I'm barely hanging on as it is.

I listen as her breaths even out, and I'm certain she's asleep. Then, and only then, do I allow myself to relax. Without the fear of my cock ramming her in the ass, I can enjoy how nice she feels wrapped up in my arms. She fits perfectly, like she was always meant to be here, even though that's a lie.

Leaning in, I breathe her in. She smells like a grandma, and I smile, recognizing the geranium and citrus scent. Even when she was a girl, she insisted on using the same lotion her grandma used. She doesn't just have an old soul; she has the same taste as old people too.

I fucking love that about her.

CHAPTER 14
TALYNN

Something wakes me in the middle of the night, and I try to sit up to get my bearings, but I can't. I'm pinned down by a heavy arm. Then it all comes back—the tequila, the talking, asking him to hold me. Maybe I'll be embarrassed in the morning, but I'm still buzzed, and this feels nice.

I snuggle back into him, giving myself permission to let go for a change. There's no regret or shame when he's still asleep. At least until something long and hard wedges between my ass cheeks. My eyes go wide as I realize it's his dick.

My clit tingles, and I have exactly enough alcohol still buzzing in my brain to push back against it. I swallow hard. God, it feels good, and it's been so long since I've been this close to a man.

Not since the academy when stupid Steve cheated on me with Samantha. She was blonde and had a bigger rack, two things Steve pointed out to me as if that was all the explanation I needed to understand why he stepped out on me. After that, I swore off men.

Not a hard thing to do when you've either dated, arrested, or grew up with every man in town.

Still hearing Colt's rhythmic breathing, I allow myself to push against him again, dragging his hard length along my core. My nipples harden, desperately wanting the hand spread across my lower abdomen to be kneading my tender breasts instead.

That's enough, Tal. It's creepy to grind against an unconscious man.

I sigh, trying to will myself back to sleep, but it's no use. My body is awake and alive.

If I were being respectful, I'd move to my side of the bed and leave him alone. Going against my hormones, I scoot forward an inch, but his arm tightens around me, bringing me back flush against him. Now his shaft is pressing into my back. I don't like this nearly as much.

"You okay?" he mumbles sleepily.

"I'm fine. Sorry for wakin' you."

I shift, needing to get some distance between me

and his stiffy before I embarrass myself and get caught trying to maneuver him back between my legs. But again, his arm braces me down, and I rub my ass against him.

"What are you doin' to me, Tal?" His voice is deep and throaty. Maybe because he's half asleep or maybe because he wants me like I want him right now. I don't know.

"Sorry."

He leans in so his lips are right behind my ear, his breath tickling my neck, and whispers, "If I didn't know any better, I'd think you were grinding on my cock."

"What if I am?" It's the tequila talking. Definitely the tequila.

"Then I'd say I hope you know what you're askin' for."

With all the audacity of tequila, I reach behind me and stroke up and down his solid length. I'm not good with eyeballing measurements, but I'd say seven inches, eight maybe? Either way, it feels like a good time, and I could use that right now.

"I know exactly what I'm askin' for," I say.

"Fuck, Bug," he groans, and I release him long enough to turn around, then put my hand right back where it was before.

In my foggy brain, I know this has regret written all over it, but I don't care. I've always been the responsible one. The one who never made any decision without thinking about every possible outcome a million times. I never had the chance to let go and make stupid mistakes. I deserve one impulsive night.

"Fuck me, Colton. Please," I beg.

He studies me with an eagle eye, and I see indecision warring in his brain. I decide to make things clear by hooking my leg over his hip and kissing him. He tastes like the earthy and slightly sweet tequila we consumed, mixed with something that's uniquely Colt.

The preteen in me squees that I'm finally kissing him, all our history melting away so I can enjoy this accomplishment. I dreamed of this moment, wrote about it in my diary, and talked incessantly about it with Sarah. Now it's coming true, and it's everything I ever wanted it to be.

He allows me control for all of two seconds before he takes over, licking the seam of my lips, then plunging his tongue inside. His kiss is demanding and aggressive. All I taste is him. All I smell is him, stealing any doubts lingering in the distance.

He rolls me onto my back, settling on his knees between my legs. He wastes no time lifting the hem of my shirt and tugging it off, leaving me in just a bra. He reaches underneath me and unhooks it one-handed. I help pull it down my arms, revealing my bare breasts.

Like a man starved, he attacks me. One hand cups a breast, testing its weight while his mouth lowers to the other. His tongue paints a circle around my nipple before drawing it into his mouth, where he sucks and bites. A gush of wetness soaks my panties, and I claw at his shoulders, holding him to me as he kisses his way to my other breast.

Everything in me is desperate for this man, even my heart.

Without sober logic to stop them, the residual feelings from when I was young bubble to the surface and expose themselves. It's not generic desire I'm experiencing; it's desire for him. Only him.

"I need you," I plead.

He leaves open-mouthed kisses on his way up my chest and neck until his mouth is back at my ear. "I'm getting there. Be patient."

I whimper, and he chuckles, low and throaty, before trailing even more kisses down my body and swirling his tongue in my belly button. He pulls away long enough to tug my thong down my legs, tossing it to the side and fixing his gaze on the apex of my thighs.

I was not prepared for sex. Nothing has been trimmed, shaved, or waxed. Mortification hits me, and I try to swing my leg over him to hide, but he stops me by gripping my thighs and holding them spread wide.

"I wasn't ready for this," I say.

He drags a finger up my slit and brings it to his mouth, where he makes a show of sucking every bit of my arousal off it. "You taste ready to me."

Holy shit. Did he really do that?

I don't have time to question it before he dives in to get a taste directly from the source. He eats me out with the same intensity as his kiss. He sucks and licks, creating a divine rhythm that has my eyes rolling into the back of my head and my toes curling into the mattress.

Digging his fingers into my thighs hard enough to bruise, he latches onto my clit and sucks. I see stars. I hear angels sing. I teleport to heaven. My thighs squeeze together, clamping his head in place as my orgasm rolls through me. It's incredible, the best I've ever had, and he hasn't even fucked me yet.

"Oh, God," I say, but I'm certain it's more like a

shout because dang. This man knows what he's doing, even though I know for a fact he doesn't.

My muscles relax, and a stupid smile spreads across my face as he wipes his face on my inner thigh, his scruff scraping against my soft skin, and even that feels incredible.

He lifts onto his knees, smirking. "Feel good, Bug?"

I cover my grin. "It was all right."

"Just all right? Guess I'll have to make this next part better." He hops off the bed to push down his boxer briefs, and I nearly gasp at how beautiful he is. Long, thick, hard, and veiny, his dick is a work of art. "Ready?"

I nod, and he climbs back onto the bed to kneel between my legs. Taking himself in hand, he drags his length up and down my swollen sex, coating himself in my arousal. I want him to hurry up already, but something about his expression holds me back from urging him on. It's almost as if he's in awe, and then I remember he's a virgin.

He pushes his head inside, his eyes squeezing shut and his head falling back on his shoulders. He holds himself there for a long moment, his large Adam's apple bobbing as he swallows. Then he comes back to me and pushes in with one powerful thrust, filling me almost to the point of pain but not quite. My pussy clenches happily.

"Fuck me," he groans. "You feel so good."

Holding himself deep inside, he runs his hands up and down my thighs. I see the barely-there control he's holding onto, and my heart melts a little for him.

"It's okay," I say softly, imagining a man's first time being too much to control. He already gave me an orgasm, so I don't need more.

His eyes pop open, meeting mine. Pulling out completely, he slaps my pussy. *Ouch.* My mouth falls open, and heat climbs up my chest.

"If you think I'm gonna let this be bad for you, then you've lost your damn mind, Talynn Davis. I know I'll only get this one shot, so fuck if I'm not gonna blow your mind. Now be quiet and take my cock like a good girl."

He grips my ankles and throws one over the other, flipping me onto my stomach in a move that's never been done to me before. Gripping my bare ass cheeks, he kneads the flesh before spreading me wide. I blush and peer over my shoulder, seeing the hard set in his jaw and animalistic look in his eyes.

My pussy responds by releasing another gush of moisture. Butterflies begin a crazy dance in my stomach. I've never seen him be this assertive and dominant. It excites me not knowing what he'll do next.

"Lift up." He pulls my hips up until I'm on my knees, my chest still lowered. "Damn, look at this beautiful pussy."

Taking handfuls of my ass, he pushes his cock back inside, but he doesn't hold back this time. He fucks me fast and hard, our skin slapping together and echoing through the room. It feels so good; I moan loudly, unable to keep quiet.

I thought I knew sex; I thought I knew what it was about. But I didn't. Not even a little. Colt has demolished my entire sexual history and has no doubt ruined me for any other man. Not even my vast collection of toys can compete with how he's making me feel right now.

Leaning over my body, he grips my wrists. "I was lyin' when I said I wanted you quiet. I wanna hear you scream my name." He twists my arms behind me, pinning my wrists at the base of my spine and using them for purchase as he fucks me.

I'm helpless in this position, unable to move even an inch. He has complete control over me. I wait for panic to set in, but it doesn't. Instead, it turns me on more. I want him to take charge. I want to be at his mercy—a power I've never given to anyone.

My cheek scrapes against the itchy sheet as he pounds into me, tilting his hips to drive into that spot that makes me wild. I'm close, so fucking close. A tsunami is heading toward me, and I can't wait for the rush.

"Oh, God. Yes." My words are muffled with my face pressed into the mattress.

"You better scream my name when you come. Let me hear it." He releases my wrists to wrap an arm around my middle and force me to my knees. Once upright, he reaches a hand between my legs and pinches my clit while his other hand squeezes a breast.

"Colt. Shit. I'm coming!" I shout, not holding back. How could I? I have no authority over my body. At this moment, I belong to him.

Tingles spread all over my body, and I nearly black out in pleasure. I don't know how long it lasts. A minute? Five? A lifetime? I have no idea, but what have I been doing all my life when I could've been experiencing this?

He carries me through my release, slowing as my body goes limp. I take deep inhales of air, trying to catch my breath. I wasn't even the one doing all the work, yet I feel as though I ran a marathon.

What the hell was that?

CHAPTER 15
CROW

I guide her back to the mattress, pulling out only long enough to roll her onto her back, then I'm back inside her, fucking her slower this time.

I knew it would be hard to keep myself together when I first entered her, but I wasn't prepared for how grueling it was. Then she gave me that pitiful look like I was some kinda teenage boy nutting off for the first time, and resolve came over me like I've never felt before.

There was no way I was gonna do anything except give her the ride of her life, and judging by the fact that she nearly came out of her skin when she came, I think I did an okay job for the first time.

I was worried I'd been too rough, but each time I

slapped her ass or talked dirty to her, her pussy creamed for me.

My Bug likes to be dominated.

Leaning over her body, I take her mouth again, wanting to get as many kisses as I can before this is over. At some point, she'll remember who I am and what she thinks I did. I'll go back to being the bad guy, and she'll go back to treating me like the shit on the bottom of her shoe.

My tongue slides along hers, and I reach down to cup her fat tit that spills over my hand. Everything about her drives me fucking crazy. I'm obsessed with every inch of her goddess-like body. I can't get enough of her soft curves, ample ass, and goddamn, these tits. But I've prolonged this enough. She's slipping away, exhausted after the fucking she just took.

"You feel so good," I murmur in her ear.

She runs her nails up and down my back, making goosebumps pop up. "Show me how good."

I hitch her thigh up, allowing me to sink even deeper and relishing how well we fit together. She clenches down, making things even snugger and driving me wild.

Shit, that's it. Just. Like. That.

Holding her gaze, I grind into her, my balls tightening until I worry they'll crawl inside. Pressure builds, and I'm seconds away from coming.

I wait until the last possible second and pull out. Rising to my knees, I pump my cock and aim for her tits. She bites on the tip of a finger, watching my cock like maybe she wants to suck on it. If there was ever going to be a next time, I'd look forward to that possibility. But as things stand, I know there won't be.

I let out a guttural curse as thick, white ropes of cum land on her creamy breasts, painting her in me. Squeezing the tip, I milk every drop, all energy leaving my body along with it. But I'm not an asshole, so I climb off the bed and wet a washcloth with warm water in the bathroom before returning and wiping it off.

Her eyes were droopy after I came, so I'm not surprised to find her asleep. Everything in me wants to pull her naked body against me so I can hold her 'til morning, but she's a ticking timebomb. She'll regain her God-given sense when she wakes up, and there'll be hell to pay. Might as well not make it worse by cuddling her.

Despite knowing all that, I have a smile on my face as I drift back to sleep. One night with Talynn is better than a lifetime with someone else.

She's gone when I wake up. Not a surprise. I'm sure she's pitching a fit as she waits for the truck to get fixed. I'll let Fred deal with her until I have myself a shower.

The water's lukewarm at best, but it gets the job done, and fifteen minutes later, I'm dressed and out the door. As suspected, I find Talynn kicking up rocks outside the gas station, pacing back and forth like a caged tiger. Her lips purse when she spots me, hands on her hips and an argument on the tip of her tongue.

I'm not an idiot, so I bypass her and head straight to the car bay, where I find Fred underneath the hood.

"How's she lookin'?" I ask.

"Good. Just about got 'er done."

"Someone inside that I can pay?"

"Yeah. Martha's in there."

Three hundred dollars and twenty minutes later, we're back in the truck. Tal hasn't said shit to me, and I don't plan on speaking either. At least not until I can get a read on her. But if I know anything since having her back in my life, it's that she can't bite her tongue for long. Something she proves when we're twenty miles down the road.

"I was drunk last night, so don't think what happened meant anything." Her arms are folded, and her legs are crossed. I'm not an expert in body language, but I'm pretty sure she's telling me I ain't ever seeing her naked again.

Damn shame.

"I know."

"Do you have any diseases?"

I had a feeling she was gonna ask about that, too, because in my lust-fueled, tequila-drunk head, I didn't wear a condom. At least I had the sense to pull out. Not that it's a foolproof method, but it's something.

"No. You know that was my first time. Maybe I should be asking you the questions," I say.

"I don't sleep around, and I've never done *that* without protection."

I didn't think she did. The woman is wound so tight, I wouldn't be surprised if she made her past partners double wrap it.

"Good to know."

"Honestly, I can't even believe you let that happen. You know how I feel about you and that I'd been drinkin'."

"Whoa, whoa, whoa. Hold your horses on that thought, Bug."

"Don't call me that. You don't get a nickname."

I squeeze the bill of my ball cap to keep from squeezing her pretty throat. "I had more to drink than you did, and I'm not the one who instigated last night."

Her face screws up, her fingernails digging into her arm. "It was a stupid mistake, and I don't want to talk about it ever again."

"Fine by me." I turn on the radio, letting Johnny Cash's voice cool my temper and hopefully hers too because we need to be on the same page soon to get through the day alive.

I make a pitstop to grab a breakfast sandwich at the first Dallas exit. Talynn rejects my offer of food but does accept a cheap cup of coffee. The bacon grease and the croissant settle my stomach and get me right again. Thank God. Dealing with drug dealers while having a hangover doesn't sound smart.

"You should call him. Find out where we're meeting," I say.

She gets her cellphone out and puts it on speaker. Good. I want to hear the fucker's voice I'm most likely gonna kill today. My Glock is in the glovebox, itching to end that asshole's life. Talynn doesn't know I'll be carrying, and I don't plan on telling her. If things go the way I want, she won't see what happens when you fuck with the people I love. And I love Henry like a brother.

For more than ten years, he and I were never apart. We didn't keep anything from each other, ever. Maybe we didn't keep in touch after I got locked up, but it doesn't change our connection. I've done a lot worse for him than kill the fucker who's blaming him for his own stupidity. Even I have enough sense not to give an addict a bunch of heroin and expect it to go over well.

"Yeah," Dario answers.

"I'm in town. Where do we meet?" Tal asks.

He gives her an address that she furiously types in her notes app.

"I'll be there in a half-hour. Don't be late," he warns.

"I won't." She's careful with her words, not letting on that she won't be alone. Good girl.

She hangs up and tosses her phone in her bag.

"He know you're a cop?" I ask.

"Yes. He knows where I live, what I do for a living, everything."

"What?" My tone is sharp.

"He made sure I knew that he wouldn't stop at killing Henry if I didn't get the cash."

"Fuck." That solidifies my decision to take him

out. There's no way I'm letting him walk this earth with that much information.

"Listen, I think you should wait outside. If things—"

"Not a fuckin' chance, Bug."

She scowls at me, whether because I used the nickname or because I'm not going along with her plan, I don't know. Doesn't matter either way.

"He'll see you as a threat," she protests.

"Good. I am a fuckin' threat."

"What if he"—her voice cracks, and she clears her throat—"what if he hurts Henry because I didn't come alone?"

"He won't get the chance."

"You don't know that."

"I do know that. I know it's asking a lot, but can you please trust me with this?"

She doesn't agree, but she doesn't argue either. I'll take it as a win.

With five minutes to spare, we pull up to an abandoned warehouse. It's a two-story brick building decorated in graffiti, the windows blown out, and a broken chain on the steel front doors.

"You got the cash?" I ask.

She pulls a tote bag out of her backpack. "It's all here."

"We'll do the exchange, and then I want you to grab Henry and get him out of there. I'll be right behind you, yeah?"

"Okay."

Her spine straightens, and she squares her shoulders, a posture she must've learned from all her policing. The same woman who dresses like she's going to Woodstock and treats her plants like her children is a motherfucking badass, and it makes me proud as hell.

We get out of the truck, and while she's inspecting the building, I quickly open the passenger door and tuck my Glock in the waistband of my jeans. Thankfully, she doesn't notice. I wouldn't put it past her to arrest me for carrying the thing since I'm a felon.

Catching up to her, I pull open the door before she can, wanting to be the first one in the building. The inside of the warehouse is just that. Must've been a manufacturing plant at some point because large machines and conveyor belts are scattered around the large space. The smell of mold and rust burns my nostrils.

Talynn gasps when she steps out from behind me and sees Henry slumped over a chair, his wrists bound together, his face unrecognizable, and his ankle twisted in an unnatural position. But my focus is on the man holding a gun to his head—dark beady eyes, a long nose, and black hair slicked to his head.

"Thought I told you to come alone," Dario barks out, and the two goons standing on either side of him take a step forward.

"Wouldn't be a fair fight since you didn't come alone," I say.

"You said not to bring another cop and I didn't," Talynn interjects, holding up the bag. "I brought the money. Let's get this over with."

The asshole nods to one of the goons who steps forward. I yank the bag from Talynn and hold it out. There's no way I'm letting any of these guys get close to her.

The one with a gun to Henry's head kicks the chair over, sending Henry to the ground like a sack of potatoes. Talynn runs over, quickly untying his hands while whispering soothing words. Keeping my eyes on all three of them, I lift Henry to his feet. He groans, blood and spit dripping from his mouth.

"Get him out of here." I toss Henry's arm over her shoulder.

"No one's going anywhere until I count the money," Dario says.

"They're waitin' in the truck." My tone brooks no debate.

Talynn nods, doing her best to carry as much as his weight as she can. Henry tries too, dragging the foot with the broken ankle behind him.

One of the goons walks over to a table and takes the brick of money out, stacking the hundreds in piles of ten. He moves quickly, like he's done it a time or two before.

"Who are you?" Dario assesses me with his head cocked to the side.

"A friend," I say. "Who the fuck are you?"

He laughs at my nerve.

"It's all here, boss," the goon says, stacking the money back up.

"Looks like it's your lucky day. If I were you, I'd take your friends home and not allow that piece of shit Henry anywhere near Dallas again, or next time, I'll go after Talynn instead. She's a feisty bitch, huh? We know how to handle a woman like that." He turns to his buddies, chuckling. "Turn her into a cum slut, shoving our cocks in each of her—"

He doesn't finish that thought before his body hits the ground, a gunshot to the head. I don't trust Henry to not fuck up again, and there's not a chance in hell I'll take the risk of him coming after Tal.

I immediately shift my aim to the goon on the right and fire before he can draw his own weapon, a look of shock immortalized on his ugly ass face. I'm not so lucky with the goon on the left. When I look over, he has one hand gripping the bag of cash and the other wrapped around the butt of a pistol, his aim on me.

I run and duck behind a conveyor belt, wincing when a shot nearly clips the top of my head. I wait for his next round to hit before popping up and squeezing the trigger. Missing, I crouch back down, hearing the loud *tink* of his round hitting the metal on the other side of the machine.

He can't leave unless he passes by me, and I can't leave without getting in his crosshairs.

We're at a standstill.

CHAPTER 16
TALYNN

Gunshots sound, putting me on alert. Shit. Colton.

My instinct is to draw my weapon and check it out, but I can't. Since I was already doing something stupid by exchanging money for my brother from a drug dealer, I didn't want to compound the situation by using my service weapon if anything went wrong.

"I need to go check it out," I say, staring through the windshield. I can't bring myself to look at Henry; it hurts too much. His face is so swollen and bruised that I wouldn't know it was him if it weren't for the tattoos on his arms.

I can't think about that right now, though. Colton is in there, possibly bleeding out.

"Stay here," Henry says on a labored exhale.

"It'll take a second. I need to make sure Colt is okay." I hop out of the truck. "Just stay here."

My hands feel empty as I walk on light feet to not be heard. There hasn't been a gunshot in almost a minute. I'm either walking into four dead bodies or a standoff. I don't know which one I'm rooting for.

Peering in through the one-inch opening of the door, I see a man on the ground. It's Dario. Shifting positions, I see another body. This one belongs to one of the goons. Colton and the third goon are missing.

How did Colton get ahold of a gun? There was a brief second that he stalled at the truck before we entered the building. I didn't think much of it at the time because I was focused on getting to Henry. Did he bring one with him?

I close my eyes and shake my head because either way, this is bad. So very bad. I should call it in right now. Get the cops here and suffer whatever consequences.

Colton can pretty much kiss the rest of his life goodbye. The third goon wouldn't have shot Dario and the other. It had to be Colton.

Being a felon, he's not even supposed to have a gun. There'll be no leniency with his history. I feel a pang of guilt because I'm the reason he's here in the first place. But I didn't ask him to bring a gun, and I didn't want anyone to die over this.

As for my involvement, I don't know what this will mean for me. Daddy is going to kill me, that's for sure. He'll have to fire me because this will not look good for his reelection. The job I love so much will be gone.

I can't worry about this right now. No. Right now, I need to make sure Colton is alive.

My heart races, something that never happens when I'm on the job. I'm unprotected in every way. No vest, no gun, nothing. But Henry and I are sitting ducks without knowing what's going on. That third goon could come out shooting at any moment.

If I could see inside, I'd know whether we should run or call an ambulance.

I push the door open slowly to avoid the rusted hinge from squeaking. Still, I only see the two dead bodies. I need to get inside. Squeezing through the door, I spot Colton hiding on the other side of a large piece of machinery.

"Get the fuck out, Tal. Now," he roars with more fury in his tone than I thought he was capable of.

I'm affronted until I scan to the other side of the room, and everything becomes clear. The second goon has a gun aimed right at me. My hands go up instinctually, but by the sinister sneer that spreads across his thin lips, that's not what he wants.

"Sorry about this," he says in a tone that tells me he is not sorry.

"For what?" I ask, even though I know the answer. He's going to kill me.

I hope Henry gets the help he needs. I hope Daddy can recover from another loss. I hope someone waters my plants.

"Bang," he says, and my vision narrows on him pressing down on the trigger.

I squeeze my eyes shut, not wanting to see it happen. The gun fires, and my body jerks back. The sound is loud, echoing in this big space full of metal. I wait for the pain, ready myself for the shock of it.

It never comes.

Blinking my eyes open, I realize I'm still standing. I look down, checking for blood. Patting around, I conclude I wasn't the one shot.

But I heard the gunfire. I saw his finger squeezing the trigger.

"Come on. We gotta get outta here." Colt grabs my arm and tugs on me. Except my feet won't move, my hands won't lower.

What just happened?

"Tal, come on. We gotta go." His tugging is more persistent now. Doesn't matter; I'm still in shock.

That's when I see the goon on the ground, the side of his head gone. Nothing but a bloody, gaping wound remains.

"Shit," Colt yanks his hat off and scrubs a hand over his head before positioning it back in place. My feet leave the ground, and I'm lifted into Colt's arms. "It's all right, darlin'. Everything's gonna be just fine, you hear me?"

"They're all dead," I deadpan.

"Yeah, they are. Don't worry about all that. Important thing is you're safe, and Henry's alive."

I nod, too shocked for anything more.

Colt opens the driver's side door and sets me in the truck. "Scoot over, okay?"

Mindlessly, I move down the bench seat. Through swollen barely-there slits for eyes, Henry watches me.

"She okay?" he asks, his voice scratchy and painful sounding.

"She'll be fine." Colt slides behind the steering wheel and starts the truck.

Something about him backing up and turning around brings me back to myself. We shouldn't be leaving. We need to call the cops.

"Stop," I say.

"What?" Colt asks.

"I said stop."

"Not happenin'. Somebody might've heard all the shots. Cops could be on their way now."

"Exactly. You killed three men. We have to report it."

"That's not gonna happen." His tone is absolute.

"I'm serious, Colt. Stop the truck right now."

"Tal, listen to me when I say there's no chance in hell I'm doin' that."

Maybe I'm still not myself because I shift to the side and hit him. Over and over, I slap him—his shoulder, his arm, his leg, his face—everywhere I can reach while screaming, "Stop the fucking car, Colt! Stop it now."

On squealing tires, he pulls to the side of the road. "What the fuck is wrong with you?"

"You left the crime scene. You made us accessories to murder. Haven't you fucked our lives up enough?"

"I *saved* your life, Tal. If it wasn't for me, you'd be dead on the ground!" he shouts right back.

"No one would've gotten shot if you weren't there."

This wasn't supposed to happen. We were trading my brother for cash. This was all my fault. I ignored my cop instincts and let emotion get in the way. It was single-minded of me to think this would go smoothly.

But we were almost out of there. I had Henry in the truck. They were letting us go. Except Colt insisted on staying. I let him decide our plan.

I meet Colt's dark brown eyes, and I know. He's the reason this went wrong. He's the reason everything goes wrong. How did I ever think it was a good idea to involve him in my life? I'm so stupid, so incredibly stupid.

"You have no fuckin' clue went down before you came back in." His mouth is tight with fury.

"You're right, and I don't want to. I can't testify against you if I know. We need to go back."

"You won't have to testify because no one will ever know."

"Talynn." Henry's weak and panting voice interrupts our argument.

Turning to him, I see sweat has broken out across his brow, and his breaths are labored. "What's wrong?"

"I need a hospital. Can't breathe."

I lift his shirt. His ribs are badly bruised. No doubt a few are broken. One could've punctured his lung.

"Take us to the hospital," I say.

Colt stares us both down, indecision in his eyes.

"I swear to God, Colt. If you don't take us to the hospital now, I will call for one myself." I reach into my bag and grab my phone.

"Fine," he says and presses on the gas so hard, we all jerk back.

I glare at him before turning back to Henry. His hand is the only uninjured thing I see on him, so I grasp it. "Hang on a bit longer, okay?"

"Don't turn him in." Spittle flies out of his mouth with the strain speaking puts on him.

"We'll worry about that after we get you looked at."

"No, Tal." His eyes bore into me. "He saved my life."

"That's debatable."

His hand squeezes mine with more force than he should have in his condition. "Promise me."

"The only thing that's important is getting you healthy."

"Promise me," he repeats.

"Yeah, okay. I promise." It's a lie, though. There's DNA evidence all over that crime scene. I touched the door to the barn, Henry bled all over the dirt, and Colt's bullets are embedded in those men.

Even if I don't report it, the cops will know. All

three of us have fingerprints and DNA recorded in the system. Colt and Henry from being arrested, and me from being a cop.

"Let me go get help," Colt says, pulling into the ER drop-off lane.

Henry drifts off while we wait, and I settle his head on my lap, a hand pressed to his back to feel for his breaths. Minutes later, Colt reappears with three hospital staff and a stretcher. Things go fast after that. He's loaded onto the gurney, and they rush him inside, me trailing behind.

"What happened to him?" a doctor asks, putting a stethoscope into his ears.

I wrap my arms around myself. "He's a drug user, and he couldn't pay. They did this as punishment."

Not a lie.

"Who are you to him?"

"His sister."

A nurse places an arm around me. "Let's let the doctors work. I'll take you to the waiting room."

I nod, turning away. Seeing them put all those tubes and needles in him is too much. My stomach lurches, and the nurse holds my hair back as I throw up into a trash can. After a stop to the bathroom to rinse my mouth out, I'm led into a cold and sterile room with a TV in the corner playing a sitcom.

"The doctor will come find you when he knows more, okay?" the nurse asks.

I nod, and then I'm alone, realizing I lost Colt somewhere along the way. Of course he left me alone to deal with this.

Everything hits me all at once, and I dissolve into tears. I wish I could go back in time and do things the right way. I'd tell Daddy, let the cops handle the dirty work, and then everything wouldn't be so fucked right now.

Except I don't know if that's true because I don't know if Colt was forced to shoot those men. It's easy to blame him; I've done it with everything else. He's been my scapegoat for as long as I can remember. It wasn't fair of me then, and it's not fair of me now.

Flashes of what we did last night come back to me. I might've been tipsy, but I knew what I was doing. I had a crush on him at six, an attraction to him at twelve, but none of that went away, no matter how much I hate him. My body doesn't seem to feel the same as my brain.

I was stupid to give in to my desires, no matter how good it felt. He's a complication. Plain and simple.

My phone chirps, and I dig it out of my bag. It's Daddy, texting to see if I'm feeling any better after calling in sick today. It's time to come clean. Too much has happened, and I don't know what to do.

I need my Daddy.

"Hey, sickie. How are you feelin'?"

Hearing his voice chokes me up, but I swallow it down so I can get it all out. I'll give him credit. He stays silent as I spill the entire situation—minus my sins at the hotel—only grunting or chuffing now and then. I'm slumped over by the time I finish, holding my head up with a hand, drained of all energy.

"What hospital are you at?" he asks.

"University Medical Center."

"I'm on my way. Don't do or say anything to anyone until I get there. You hear?"

"Yes, sir."

"Sit tight."

The line goes dead, and I stuff my phone back in my bag. I spot movement from the corner of my eye and see Colt standing in the doorway, hands tucked in his pockets.

"Can I sit?" he asks.

CHAPTER 17
CROW

I don't take the chair next to her, keeping a spot between us. It feels right to give her some room.

"I went back and cleaned up," I say.

Her incredulous glare tells me she's not happy with that decision. "You did what?"

"Wiped away all trace of us being there. It's all gone: fingerprints, Henry's blood, the tire tracks, and footprints." I offer her the small bag full of cash. "And I got this back."

"Why would you do that?" she asks, not taking the bag.

I set it on the chair between us. "I didn't think any of us wanted to go to prison, for one."

"I haven't made up my mind about reportin' everything."

Guess Henry's request wasn't enough for her. Nothing's ever enough for her. I'm certain not even the truth from twenty years ago would be enough for her. She'd find a reason to hate me no matter what. And fuck. Why does that hurt? I shouldn't give a shit about her. But I do. Ain't that a bitch.

"Do you even want to know what happened in there?" I ask.

She considers with pursed lips. "Tell me."

"Dario was talkin' shit about how next time Henry fucks up, he'll take it up with you. He said some fucked up shit I won't repeat, and I don't know about you, but I don't trust that Henry won't fuck up again. I hope he doesn't. I hope this was a wake-up call, but after everything you've told me about him, I'm not sure. I couldn't let anything bad happen to you, Bug. Even if you hate my guts."

If I thought that would soften her up, I was wrong.

"So you shot him?" she accuses. "Over a threat?"

"Hell yeah, I shot him for that, and I'd do it again."

"I can't believe you. This isn't the Wild West. You can't go around killin' people because they say something you don't like," she hisses.

"We live in two different worlds, Bug."

"You're wrong. It's the same world. You just don't follow the rules."

I don't respond because it's the truth. Going to prison taught me a lot of things, including that the authorities can't be trusted. The last five years with the club only solidified my opinions. Most cops don't give a shit about right or wrong; they're only looking out for themselves.

"What happened after that?" she asks.

"The other two reached for their weapons. I took one of them out, and you know what happened with the other. Whether or not you want to admit it, I saved your life."

She mulls that over while I stare at the wall. I won't apologize for any of it, including cleaning up the scene. Truthfully, I didn't trust Talynn to listen to Henry, so after we got him to the hospital, I had to choose. Go inside with them or head back and fix this mess. I couldn't help Henry, but I could help all three of us and keep us out of trouble.

It was an obvious choice.

"Has a doctor been in to see you?" I ask.

"Not yet." She sighs. "My dad's on his way here. I told him everything."

Fuck.

When I first got let out on parole, Sheriff Davis

stopped by to *welcome* me back to town. I was surprised at how fair he treated me. He told me I'd face some trouble from the town—which I expected—but if I stayed on the right side of the law, the department would leave me alone. That didn't turn out to be true after Talynn found out, but I don't fault him for that.

Something tells me what happened today'll send him over the edge, and I'll no longer have that courtesy.

"He pissed?" I asked.

"I don't know. He told me to sit tight, and he'd be here soon, then hung up."

Our conversation is interrupted when a doctor in a white coat and a stethoscope around his neck steps inside the room.

"Miss Davis?" he asks.

"That's me."

We both stand, but only Talynn approaches the doctor. I'm sure she doesn't want me in her space right now.

"Your brother is alive but just barely. He sustained numerous injuries, including severe head trauma, multiple broken ribs, a broken ankle—as you already know—and his lung is punctured, which we've already treated. We're taking him back to surgery now. We need to perform a craniotomy to relieve the pressure on his brain. If he tolerates that, then we'll fix his ankle."

Talynn sniffles and wipes tears from her eyes. It's all I can do to not wrap her up in my arms and comfort her.

"Will he be okay?" she asks.

"He has a tough road ahead. His body was already weak from extensive drug use and malnourishment, so I won't make any promises. But we'll do everything we can." The doctor sets a hand on her shoulder, and I home in on the touch.

Talynn is the most beautiful woman in the world. There's no way the decent-looking doctor with no wedding ring hasn't noticed, but I swear to Christ, if he doesn't remove his motherfucking hand, I'll do it for him.

"Thanks, Doc. You better get to it." I sidle up to Talynn and put an arm around her waist.

The doc's smile falters, and he drops his hand. *That's what I thought, fucker.*

"Right. I'll check back in after surgery." He turns and leaves.

"What are you doing?" Talynn shakes me off.

"He was hittin' on you. It was unprofessional."

"He wasn't hittin' on me; he was comforting me."

"No. He wasn't."

"Even if he was, I'm not your concern."

I'm sure by everyone else's standards, she's right. But I claimed her last night, and that changes everything. No more being the Davis family fall guy. Henry better live so two things can happen. First, so I can kick his ass for putting his sister through all this shit, and second, so I can clear my name and fix all that's broken between me and Tal.

"Just lookin' out for you."

"Well, don't."

"Yes, ma'am," I sass.

"You know what? You should go. Daddy will be here soon, and I'm sure you're the last person he wants to see."

"I can wait."

"I was trying to be polite, but since you can't take a hint, I'm asking you to leave. Now," she snaps and reclaims her seat, pulling out her phone and tapping away at the screen.

Knowing this isn't a battle I'll win, I tuck my hands in my pockets and ask, "Can you please text me and let me know how he does?"

I expect her to tell me no and that it's not my business, but she doesn't.

"Sure." I'm nearly out the door when she adds, "Colt?"

"Yeah?"

"For however messed up things got today, I appreciate you volunteerin' to help. You didn't have to do that."

"Welcome."

I pull my phone out of my back pocket, only to see no messages. Tucking it back in, I get back to mucking stalls.

Usually, I leave my phone in the cabin while I work because before now, no one except my brothers had my number, and they knew where to find me. But Talynn also has my number, and since I left her at the hospital two days ago, I've been carrying my phone everywhere, waiting to hear from her.

My pride hasn't allowed me to be the first to reach out, but even that's waning. I tell myself if I haven't heard from her by tonight, I'll text. Or maybe call. I haven't decided.

"Any news?" Sin asks, leaning over the gate of the stall I'm in.

"Nah, man. Nothin' yet."

"She's probably punishing you for going all Rambo on those motherfuckers."

I told Sin all about what went down. He was pissed I didn't ask him to come as backup but understood it would've been more than Deputy Davis could handle.

"Maybe." I toss another shovel's worth of shit into the wheelbarrow.

"Probably better off this way, bro. You don't need to be makin' friends with cops."

I may have left out the part where I fucked Talynn good and hard while we were away. It's better no one knows that part.

"Yeah. Prolly right about that too."

"I know I am. Wouldn't be good if she popped by at the wrong time and saw things she shouldn't."

I don't respond because, no shit. Even if everything went my way and I proved to Talynn I'm not who she thinks I am, our worlds don't mix. She only sees black and white, right and wrong. There's no chance I could get her to look the other way about club business.

She doesn't see the good the club does. Small towns are gold mines for drug and gang activity, and we make sure none of that settles in Diamond. The guns we run aren't sold locally. Most of them are sent over the border to Mexico. Not that it matters because this is Texas, and everyone has a gun. But she wouldn't see it like that.

"You ready for tonight?" he asks.

"Yeah."

We got a shipment heading to the border. As much as I'd like to sit around and wait for my phone to ring, there's business to be done.

He pounds a beat on the wooden gate. "All right. See you later then."

Once the horses are settled, I head to my cabin to wash the shit stink off me and have a quick dinner. After that's done, I run out of things to keep my mind busy, and I'm back to watching my phone.

This is fucking stupid. She's obviously not gonna call, and I need to know if Henry made it out of surgery. I dial her number and listen to it ring, expecting to be sent to voicemail.

"Hello?" she answers.

"Tal, hey. How are you?"

"I'm okay." She sounds fucking tired and sad.

"How's Henry?"

"He didn't make it," she chokes out, and my stomach sinks.

"Fuck." I blow out a breath. "I'm so sorry, Tal."

I listen to her cry for a long minute, wishing like hell I could be there for her.

"Is there anything I can do?" I ask.

"Do?" she asks incredulously. "No, Colt. There's nothing you can do."

"Listen—"

"No, you listen. His death wasn't your fault, but that doesn't change the fact that you're attached to every single loss I've ever suffered. Even hearin' your voice brings back the pain I felt each time. So if you want to *do* something, don't call, don't show up at my house, just stay away."

"Tal, that's not fair."

"Life isn't fair. If it were, I'd still have both my brothers and my momma." With that, she hangs up.

I scrub a hand down my face and lean back in my dining room chair. My childhood best friend is dead, and the one woman my brain and dick have latched on to wants nothing to do with me.

Life was so much easier on the inside. Fuck. Never thought I'd say that.

Tal was right about one thing. Life isn't fair.

CHAPTER 18
TALYNN

Henry's funeral is quiet and peaceful. We only invited a few people to the graveside service, mostly neighbors, a few distant relatives, and of course, Sarah.

Dressed in his Sunday best, Daddy stands strong, head held high, as we listen to our preacher deliver a message of hope. Sarah is in a long black, flowy dress, gripping my hand tight, tears running a river down her cheeks.

To the right of the fresh plot are Momma and Ben's graves. The sight of the three lined up in a neat row kills me, and I break down in an epic mess of snotty tears. Daddy's arm drapes over my shoulders, giving me support. He doesn't look down at me, and I know it's because he's doing his best to keep his own emotions in check.

One by one, we pluck roses from the arrangement on Henry's closed casket—he was in too rough of shape for it to be open—and say our final goodbyes. When it's my turn, I pull a yellow rose and whisper a promise to take care of Daddy, that I'll make him proud he was my brother, and that I'll keep his memory alive. Dropping it down into the hole, I blow him a kiss and turn to leave.

After a tearful goodbye, Sarah drives off, and I take Daddy's arm. As we're walking to his truck, I catch a flash of black out the corner of my eye. A shadowy figure stands in the distance behind some trees. It could've been anyone, but I know who it is when I spot the motorcycle parked behind him.

Colton.

I don't know how to feel about him being here. The sane part of me is glad he has the chance to say goodbye. But the emotional, angry side wants to chase him off.

Rationally, I know he's not bad luck and that if God wants to call His soldiers home, He will. But the mere sight of Colt has me wanting to bubble wrap Daddy, just in case.

"Talynn," Daddy prompts, holding the door open.

"I'm comin'." With one last glance at Colt, I get in the truck.

"You talked to him since the hospital?" Daddy asks, steering the truck toward home.

"Who?"

"Don't play dumb with me. We both know that boy was up on the hill."

"He's not a boy anymore, Daddy."

"I know." He runs his hands up and down the steering wheel. "You never did say why you went to him when things got out of hand for Henry."

Hearing my brother's name sends another pang through my heart. I know the only reason he's in the ground right now is because of his choices, but it doesn't make it easier to lose him.

"I thought I had a better chance of a good outcome if I didn't involve the law," I say.

"You *are* the law."

I pinch the bridge of my nose. "I know, but I couldn't be in that moment. Colt felt like the safest option."

"I don't know how to feel about knowin' there are three dead bodies up there, but I can't do anything about it because it'll implicate my own daughter."

"I don't know how to feel about it either. All I can say is I know how it went down, and my conscience is clear. My only mistake was trustin' him and not you."

"I think Colt did what he had to do to keep you safe," Daddy says.

My head cocks to the side. "You're defendin' a murderer?"

"I've seen murderers. That man ain't one of 'em."

I can't believe what I'm hearing. It makes no sense. Even if he doesn't consider the drug dealers' lives worth anything, Colt killed Ben. It doesn't matter if it was an accident. He still did it.

"How can you say that?"

"Those bikers don't follow our rules. It's best you remember that. In their world, they are judge, jury, and executioner, all in the blink of an eye. From what I understand, the men he shot had bad intentions for you, and I'm glad I don't have to worry about them crawlin' out the gutter to pay you back for something Henry did."

"So it's okay for him to take the law into his own hands?"

One bushy brow lifts. "You did. You never should've been there and given those men money in exchange for your brother's life."

My head hangs. "I know, but no one died when I was in that room."

"You have no idea what would've happened if Colt hadn't been there. They could've killed you and Henry. Then what would I be left with." He tilts my chin up. "All I'm sayin' is both of you made mistakes in an impossible situation. Don't judge lest ye be judged."

"Great. Now you're quotin' the Bible?"

"I love you, Talynn."

"I love you too." I glance over at the three plots of land that hold my family. "I miss them."

"Me too, kid." Daddy pulls away with a sigh. "Me too."

A week later, I'm back at work. We have a new deputy, Justin, and today, I'm tasked with showing him around and how we do things in Diamond.

"A lot of this job is patrollin'. The public likes to see us around, even if we're not needed," I say to the kid sitting next to me. And I say kid because he's barely twenty-two and looks all of seventeen.

"So it's boring," Justin deadpans.

"Not always. You'll get to know everyone and build your own rhythm."

"So. . . boring."

I roll my eyes and turn up the radio. I'd rather listen to music than explain how special this town is. He'll either love it or hate it here. Nothing I say will influence him. I let my mind wander as I continue to drive around.

Everything in my life has returned to normal since the funeral. I go to work, make Daddy dinner, and fuss over my plants. Nothing has changed, but nothing feels the same. It's not that Henry was part of my daily life before he died. The opposite, really, but I knew he was out there before. Knowing he's not out there anymore makes my world feel duller.

Don't get me started on Colton. I can't bring myself to feel bad about our last interaction because everything I said was true. But tell that to my stupid head because he's living up there rent-free.

I replay all our conversations during the day, and at night, my vibrator gets a good workout as I replay the way he fucked me.

God, it was so hot. Never has a man been so attentive and determined with me. It's a damn shame it'll never happen again.

"Hungry?" I ask Justin.

"I could eat."

I take him to the Frostee, where we order burgers

and shakes before returning to the car. We make polite chitchat while we eat, but I can already tell we'll never be friends.

I'm taking my last bite of burger when a parade of motorcycles drives by at a slow roll. I scan the profile of each biker until my eyes land on the one at the tail end. Colton. He looks so sexy and masculine with his hands gripping the handlebars, his back slightly bowed, a black bandana on his head, and a dark beard. That's new. Last time I saw him, it was mere scruff.

"Who are they?" Justin asks.

"Diamond Kings MC. Technically, they're a motorcycle enthusiast club, but everyone knows they're more of a biker gang. Though they won't admit to that."

"Let's pull 'em over."

"What for?" I ask incredulously.

"That last one's tail brake light is out. See?" He points, and he's right. Colt's brake light is out.

That's when an idea hits me. Maybe I can give my Colt addiction a hit while not giving him the satisfaction of knowing how much I've been thinking about him. It's my job, after all.

"Light 'em up," I say and pull onto Main, speeding up until I'm directly behind Colt.

His eyes go to his side mirror before he glances over his shoulder. He mouths the word "shit," flips on his turn signal to pull onto the side of the road, and waves the guys in front of him ahead. One by one, they glance back, all with a look of apprehension.

No idea what that's about. I've already decided I'll give Colt a warning and send him on his way.

I park behind him, noticing how he turns off the ignition and positions his hands on the handlebars, not moving an inch. Apparently, the other members have clued him in on proper etiquette when being pulled over.

Justin and I get out of the car, me approaching him on his left and Justin on his right.

"Do you know why I pulled you over?" I ask.

Colt's eyes devour me from head to toe, like maybe he's been thinking about me too. That thought gives me a thrill.

"I don't, Deputy Davis," he drawls.

"Your brake light is out," Justin chimes in with such a condescending attitude that I want to tell his ass to wait in the car.

"Who are you?" Colt asks.

"Deputy McAlister." Justin plucks at his name tag proudly. God, this kid is a dweeb.

"Thanks for tellin' me about the light. I'll get it fixed today."

"License and registration," Justin says.

"I know who he is and that he's legal," I say.

Colt gives him a smug grin. "You hear that, McAlister? She knows all about me."

I roll my eyes.

"I'm in training, and I think this'll be a good way to test my skills. So if you'll comply, we'll get you back on the road," Justin says.

"Sure, little buddy." Colt digs in his back pocket for his wallet.

Before I take my next breath, Justin's eyes go wide, and he reaches for his weapon. "Gun. He has a gun."

Shit. Why would he carry a gun in town? What an idiot. I immediately go into damage control, my mind spinning the ways I can get him out of this.

"No laws have been broken, Deputy McAlister. In case you forgot, Texas is an open carry state. Holster your weapon." I use my most authoritative tone.

"You don't know that."

"I do. Holster your weapon and go sit in the car."

Reluctantly, he secures his gun and storms to the car like a scolded child.

"He's nice," Colt says, sarcasm dripping from his tone.

"Sorry about that. He saw the broken light, and I had no good reason to say no."

"It's fine." His jaw works as he chews on a piece of gum.

I wasn't sure how he'd behave after I was so cold and heartless the last time we spoke. But apparently, he doesn't hold grudges.

"You shouldn't be carryin'."

"Probably not." He shifts his weight, fingers tapping on the top of his helmet in his lap.

"I should take you in."

"You should." He gives me a challenging look. "Are you goin' to, Deputy Davis?"

I saw at my lip while I think. He doesn't get a free pass for the rest of his life because of our history. If anything, it should make me more inclined to uphold the law. But he and I both know I won't. At least not this time.

"Just please, don't let me catch you with a weapon again. I have a job to do."

"Yes, ma'am." He salutes me, then shifts his gaze to across the street. "You doin' okay? After. . . you know?"

"I'm all right."

"That's good to know."

"Are you okay?" I ask, despite my better judgment. Why am I always letting my guard down with him? I draw clear boundaries, then plow right through them. It makes no sense.

"Deputy Davis," Justin calls out.

My head lulls back, and I close my eyes, praying to the Lord above for some patience. "Yeah?"

"I need to talk to you. Right now."

Colt grins and mock whines, "Mommy, I need help."

"Stop." I laugh, despite myself. "Be right back."

"I'll be here." He stretches his legs out and rests his hands behind his head as though he's kicking back to enjoy the day.

I storm back to the car. "What is it?"

"He's a felon. He's unlawfully carrying."

Shit. He ran his plates and found out who he was. Blood rushes to my head, whooshing in my ears. This is bad. I need to think fast because this is about to get ugly.

"Let it go, Justin. He wasn't doing anythin' wrong."

"No. He's breaking the law. I'm taking him in." Justin removes his cuffs from his belt.

"Justin, I said let it go. I'm your superior, and you will listen."

"Sorry, but you're wrong. I'm arresting him."

I am wrong, and protocol agrees. So would every other person in the department. If I push this, word will spread, which could mean trouble for Daddy and me.

Damn it. What do I do now?

CHAPTER 19
CROW

Flashbacks assault my mind as the kindergarten cop slaps cuffs on me and pats me down. The first time this happened, my hands were shaking, and I all but pissed myself. I was terrified, and everyone looked at me like I was the biggest piece of shit on earth.

I'm fucking furious with myself for being so careless, but we were heading on a run, and it's not smart to leave yourself unprotected. Especially when you're meeting at the border. Shit can go sideways in a heartbeat, and I wouldn't have time to grab a weapon from one of my brothers.

McAlister reads me my rights before roughly shoving me into the back of Tal's car. I'm fucked. So goddamned fucked, I can't even process it. News of three drug dealers found shot in a warehouse hit the news a few days ago. According to reporters, there were no leads. But the second my gun is processed, they'll link me to the murders, and I'll never be a free man again.

"Fuuuuuuck," I roar into the empty cop car.

I was gonna ditch the gun when I got back, but things got busy, and I spaced. One stupid mistake, and now my life is over. Again. Fuck. Fuck. Fuck.

I look out the window, taking everything in and knowing I'll never see it again. The Frostee, the park in the center of town, the trees, the ugly ass dirt that coats everything around here. I'll even miss that.

Talynn and McAlister argue in front of the car. I can't hear what they're saying but judging by Tal's angry gestures, she's delivering him a new asshole. I recognize it from all the times she's done the same to me. Yet another thing I'll never experience again. Didn't much like it when she was doing it before, but now, I'm pissed I'll never feel her fire directed at me again.

Talynn throws her hands in the air and gets in the car, slamming her door shut. McAlister is smug and confident as he strolls to the passenger side and slides in. Neither of them speaks to each other or me.

As Talynn speeds to the jail, I stare out the

window; her fury over the situation is evident. Anger bubbles low in my gut, topped with a good amount of self-loathing and desperation. Who'll take over working with the horses? Will they love them as much as I do?

Wish I could've said goodbye.

I'm glad my brothers got away. If Talynn had pulled the whole caravan over, she would've found a fuck ton more than my Glock. If there's one thing I did right in all this, it's waving them on so they weren't caught up in this bullshit.

We're at the jail too soon, and McAlister is yanking me out of the car. It's laughable how he thinks he's the one in control. Even with my hands cuffed, I could kill this motherfucker with ease. He's half my weight and a good six inches shorter. But that won't help anything, so I let him shove me.

"I need a minute," Talynn says before McAlister leads me into reception.

"That's not appropriate," the asshole bites out.

"Give me a fuckin' minute." She punctuates each word.

He thinks on it for a minute before pushing me toward her and storming through the front door of the jail.

"What a prick," she mutters. "Colton—"

"Wasn't your fault," I say.

"It is. I didn't have to pull you over."

"Then why did you?" I ask.

"Honestly?"

"This is probably the last time I'll ever see you, so yeah, fuckin' honesty would be good."

She stares at her hands that are woven together. "I don't know."

"Not good enough."

Her teeth work at her lower lip. "I had a talk with my dad. He said some things that got me thinkin', and I guess I just wanted to see you."

I scoff. "Like hell."

"I don't know why I keep putting myself in your path, okay? But I do, and that means something. There's a reason I'm drawn to you, and I want to know what that is."

"So instead of knockin' on my door, you pull me over and get me arrested?"

Her brown eyes meet mine, and I see it. She's telling the truth. In her own fucked up way, this beautiful woman cares for me. Despite all the shit she thinks I did, all the shit I actually did, and the confusion of both those things mixed, she cares for me.

Well, ain't that some shit.

"I'm so sorry. I wish I hadn't."

"Guess it doesn't matter anymore. That gun will get tied to what happened in Dallas eventually."

"Jesus Christ, Colt. It's the same gun?" she asks incredulously. "Why didn't you get rid of it?"

"I don't know. I wasn't thinkin'."

"This is bad. So bad." She places a hand on her worried forehead.

"I won't tell them you were there. This won't come down on you."

"What are you even talkin' about? You have to tell them the truth. You have to make them believe you were protecting Henry and me."

"No. Abso-fuckin-lutely not." I thought I was done protecting Talynn, but I guess I was wrong.

"At some point, Colt, you need to look out for yourself." She stands inches from me, her gaze intense on me.

"Why bother?"

Her face softens, eyes brimming with tears. "What happened to you that you don't think you're worth saving?"

I want to tell her how things changed the day Ben died. I trusted her dad when he said to keep quiet and everything would be okay. I trusted my parents when they said I was a kid and their lawyers would get me off. When neither of those things happened, and no one came to my defense, something in me died.

My life didn't mean anything to the people I trusted most in life, so why would it mean anything to me?

But I can't say that. It exposes the rawest part of me, and that can't happen. Not when I'm heading back inside. You show any weakness in there, you'll be ripped to shreds. My only defense is my tough exterior.

Besides, it's better that she doesn't know the truth.

"I'm pissed off at myself enough for the both of us, Bug. Don't need you addin' to it."

"I can't fix this, Colt. I'm so sorry."

"It is what it is. Don't worry about it."

"I'll make sure you have the best defense lawyer. I know people," she says.

"That would be much appreciated. Thank you."

We stare at each other in awkward silence, knowing this is the death of whatever we might have had.

"Guess I better get you in there before McAlister comes back out," she says, then goes back to worrying that lower lip. I home in on the movement, wanting so badly to taste her one last time.

Fuck it.

"Can I ask for one thing before we go?"

"What?"

"Kiss me goodbye."

She glances around, checking for any watchful eyes, but we're alone. Taking two steps toward me, she grips the front of my cut in both hands and tugs me the rest of the way. Lifting up on tiptoes, she crashes her lips to mine. Our teeth clash, and our tongues tangle in a kiss that isn't pretty but goddamned perfect.

Her lips are so fucking soft, and she tastes like a chocolate milkshake. I memorize all of it, knowing the second I'm inside, the only thing I'll have left are my memories.

Too soon, she's pulling away panting. "I wish it could be more."

"Me too, Bug. Me too."

CHAPTER 20
TALYNN

I storm into Daddy's office, finding him behind his old metal desk, staring at a computer screen. His office isn't fancy, but when he was first elected, I came in and decorated the best I could, hanging pictures of him shaking important people's hands, newspaper articles of good things he's done throughout his career, and even a few family portraits.

Closing the door behind me, I say, "We need to talk."

Daddy looks up, his reading glasses perched on the end of his nose. "What's up?"

"Your new recruit is out of control."

"I take it today didn't go well?" He keeps clacking away at the computer, disinterested.

"He's an asshole."

"Language," he chides.

"Sorry."

"What did Deputy McAlister do that was so bad?"

"The Diamond Kings were rollin' through town, like they do, and he noticed one of them had a broken brake light. It was a slow day, so I thought it'd be good to see how he handles traffic stops."

"Okay," he draws out, still not looking away from his screen. "I'm not seeing the problem."

"I'm gettin' there." I sit down in a plastic chair across from him. "Colt had a gun on him, and McAlister saw it when he was getting his license out."

He yanks off his glasses, giving me his full attention. "The Diamond King you pulled over was Colton?"

"Yes, and then he ran Colt through the system, saw he was a felon, and arrested him."

"Christ."

"It's the same gun he used in Dallas."

His mouth falls open, but nothing comes out.

"He said I didn't have to worry, that he'll leave me out of it." My eyes sting, but I refuse to cry. "I didn't mean for this to happen."

Daddy rests his forehead in his hands, looking way more upset than I thought he would. "Talynn, I need to tell you something."

"What?"

"There are some things you don't know." He stands and moves to my side of the desk, sitting on the edge, his body slumped like he's exhausted.

"Like what?" My mind spins, wondering what this has to do with Colt.

"Colt didn't kill Ben."

His words hit me like an atomic bomb. I can't breathe. I can't think. My head spins, and confusion sets in.

"What?"

He sits in the plastic chair next to me, taking my hands in his. "It's my fault. All of it."

"What are you talking about? I saw him with the gun." I recall that day vividly. There's no way my mind conjured up something that didn't happen.

"He had the gun, but he wasn't the one who shot it."

"Then who. . .?" Like a light clicking on in the dark, everything becomes clear. It was Henry. Why didn't I see it before now?

Henry wasn't the same after that day. He self-destructed like he was punishing himself.

Punishing himself for killing his brother.

"No. No. Daddy, no," I stammer, a lump forming in my throat.

"I'm sorry I never told you." His shoulders hunch, and he drops my hands.

"You let him go to prison for somethin' he didn't do?"

He's back on his feet, gesturing wildly. "It was his choice, Talynn."

I've never seen him like this. Daddy is always composed and steadfast, never out of control like he is now.

"He chose to spend most of his life locked up?" I can't believe what I'm hearing. Why would Colt do something like that?

"Colton was sixteen, still considered a juvenile. Henry'd just turned eighteen and had been in trouble with the law before. Even with it being an accident, there was a good chance he'd go away for a long time."

"Colt went away for a long time," I grit out.

"I didn't think the court would give him that long of a sentence. You gotta believe, I thought they'd give him a slap on the wrist because he was a decent kid, and it was an accident."

"But that's not what happened, and you still let him take the blame."

"What was I supposeda do, Talynn?" His face turns red, and veins in his neck protrude. This isn't good for his blood pressure, but I'm too consumed with hearing all the lies I've been told since I was twelve.

"Tell the truth!" I yell.

"It was too late. I woulda been fired, and it wouldn't have looked good for Henry."

"I can't believe this." I rest my head in my hands. "No wonder you went so easy on Colt when he came back to town. How did I not see this before?"

Questions flood my mind. Why didn't Colt stand up for himself back then? Why did he let this happen? How could he spend twenty years serving time for a crime he didn't commit? I don't understand.

"I deserve your anger but don't think I haven't paid for my mistakes." He chokes up and swallows hard. "I lost your momma because of what I did. God punished me in the worst way He could. He took the love of my life from me."

"You think that exonerates you?" My brows bunch, and I shoot him a look of disbelief.

"I made a horrible choice, Talynn, but I thought I could make it up to him once he got out. It's why I told you to leave him alone."

"Oh my God." I stand and make my way to the door. "I don't even know who you are anymore."

"I did what I thought was right for my family. I was wrong."

"So, what are you going to do about it now, Daddy? Because there's a man sittin' in the county jail right now who's about to spend the rest of his life in prison for the sins of this family."

"I don't know what I can do." He holds his hands out, palms up.

"Make this right, Daddy, or I swear to God, I will never speak to you again."

"Talynn," he calls out, but I'm already out the door.

"How did you convince them to let you talk to me?" Colt asks.

We're in one of the rooms the jail uses for lawyers to talk to their clients. Colt is in a bright orange jumpsuit, hands cuffed to the metal table separating us. Even like this, he's the sexiest man I've ever seen. The twelve-year-old girl with a crush on her brother's best friend rears her immature head.

I've spent so many years suppressing those feelings, thinking I was directing them at a killer and ashamed for it.

Now that the truth is out, I don't hold anything back.

I smile softly. "I told you I know people."

He lifts a brow in question.

"Fine." I sigh. "I dated one of the guards who ended up cheating on me, so he owed me."

"Well, shit."

"Yeah." My awkward laugh fades into silence.

"Why are you here, Bug?"

I shift in my seat, not knowing how to bring this up. Straightening my spine, I decide to just spit it out. "I know you didn't kill Ben."

He pushes as far back as the chains allow, a look of utter shock on his beautiful face. "How—"

"My dad told me."

"I wasn't even sure if he knew."

"Yeah. He knew."

He shakes his head. "I don't understand."

"What I don't understand is why *you* didn't say anything?"

He blows out a heavy breath. "I thought about it. I might've if someone had asked me what happened. But no one did."

"No one asked you for your side?"

"No. Not one person. But that wasn't the only reason."

"What do you mean?" I ask.

He stares at his feet, thinking. I wish I could climb into his head and get the truth. He's been holding so much inside I'm not sure I'll ever get the whole truth.

Finally, he straightens. "Did you know Henry was suicidal back then?"

I flinch. "No. I knew he was moody and got in trouble, but I didn't know that."

"He was always dark. His thoughts, his actions, everything was dark. Your parents were always pissed at him, and he was havin' a hard time in school because nothin' made sense to him. He thought he was stupid and hated himself for it. Right before the accident, your dad gave him an ultimatum. Either enlist or get out. But in his head, it was enlist or kill himself."

"I overheard that fight. It was bad." I remember the night Ben and I sat at the top of the stairs, eavesdropping.

"He came to my house that night, and I snuck out. He didn't say he was comin' to say goodbye, but I knew that's what it was, and I knew he had your dad's gun. I sat out in the field with him all night, just talkin' to him. Eventually, I convinced him to join the

Army. The next day he was plannin' to enlist. Your dad was so fuckin' proud. You have no idea what that did for his self-esteem."

"He was so different that day. I remember seeing him smile for the first time in forever."

"I knew it was a bad idea to play with the gun. Ben did too. He wasn't even gonna come out there with us. I think he only did so he could make sure Henry didn't do anythin' stupid."

A single tear streaks down my face, and Colt's arm jerks like he wants to wipe it away but realizes his hands are cuffed to the table. He sighs in defeat.

"He was just playin' around, spinnin' the gun around his finger, bein' an idiot. Ben was gripin' about how dangerous it was, and Henry aimed it at him. Your dad never kept his guns loaded, and Henry still had the bullets in his pocket. But he didn't know there was a round in the chamber. It was an accident."

"I wish I wasn't so nosey. It wouldn't have kept Ben alive, but it might've changed something for you."

"I doubt it. Henry handed me the gun in a panic, and instinctually, I took it."

"I'm so sorry, Colt."

He shrugs. These are all things he accepted years ago. "I knew if they found out he killed Ben—their golden boy—he wouldn't survive. He couldn't take disappointing them again."

"Even so, how could you sacrifice your life for him?" I ask.

"Your dad kept telling me I'd be okay. To keep my mouth shut and the court would see I was a good kid from a good family, and they'd let me go. Felt like the right thing to do. My parents had money and hired me some fancy lawyer who told me the same thing. But even then, no one asked me if I did it. By that time, I didn't think anyone would believe me anyway."

I'm going to be sick. This is so much worse than I thought. Why would Daddy not ask him what happened? It makes no sense.

"Colt, I'm so sorry."

"Wasn't your fault then, and it ain't your fault now."

Holy hell, is this man for real? How can he be so forgiving?

"It kind of was. If I hadn't said anything, maybe they would've—"

"Can't play that game, Bug. Shit happens."

"My dad thought because you were underage and didn't have a rap sheet, that you wouldn't go to prison. He thought maybe parole or something. I don't know."

"Everyone thought that, but the whole county lost Ben. He was a shining star in our community. I didn't stand a chance. There's no fair trial in that situation."

"I don't know what to say except I'm sor—"

"No more apologies. You want to make things right, then go and live. Forgive your dad because he's a good man. He was just protectin' his boy. I'd do the same if I had a kid." His dark eyes gloss over, and he smiles, but it's forced.

Before I can stop myself, I wrap my hands around his. They're cold and tough with deep callouses, but to me, they feel like heaven. I don't bother arguing with him about Daddy. It's not important. What is important is making sure he knows how much I appreciate the man he's always been.

"You're either stupid or incredibly kind and caring."

He smiles, and it's real this time. "I'm leanin' toward fuckin' stupid."

"You're wrong." I grin back.

His thumb strokes my hand, and that one motion is so much more intimate than anything we've shared because there are no secrets between us this time. This time, I know exactly who he is.

There's a pounding on the metal door, and I jerk my hands away right before it opens, and my asshole ex pops his head in. "Time's up."

"Two more minutes?" I ask.

"Two more. Then he's gotta go back."

The door closes, and my hands are back on his. "Hang in there, okay?"

I almost kick myself at how lame that sounds.

"I haven't given up yet." He flashes me a wolfish grin. "Besides, prison is so much easier than bein' on the outside. There's not this feisty woman who likes to make my life hell." He shivers dramatically.

Knowing I only have a minute more with him, I round the table and lift one of his arms as high as it will go, duck under it, and straddle his lap. Cupping his face, I kiss him with all the emotion building up inside of me, needing an outlet. I give it all to him, and he takes it with just as much intensity.

He pushes off my lips and trails kisses down my jaw and neck, biting and sucking, making his way to my exposed cleavage. I arch into him, loving the feel of his prickly stubble burning my already hot skin.

"You're all I'll be thinkin' about," he says between panting breaths. "These tits." He bites into my flesh. "This pussy." He thrusts his hips up, allowing me to feel his erection. "And this mouth."

He pulls away so I can bring my lips to his once again.

All too soon, I hear the heavy boots walking toward the room. I give him one last kiss and untangle myself. Three knocks sound, and the guard steps in, unaware of what happened. Or at least that's what I thought until his eyes home in on my neck and chest.

I scratch at the area. "Allergies. These damn hives won't go away."

He cocks his head. "Right."

My eyes meet Colt's as he's unhooked from the table and jerked to standing.

"See ya 'round," he says.

I nod. "I promise you will."

Even if the only way I can talk to him is during visiting hours, I swear on all things holy, I'll see him as much as I possibly can. He deserves to know that someone cares.

CHAPTER 21
CROW

"Colton Masters." A guard approaches my cell, a blank expression on his face. "Let's go. You're out of here."

My body tenses. *What the fuck?* My preliminary hearing isn't until next week. "Go where?"

"Home. Strip club. Fucking McDonalds. I don't know, and I don't care." He cuffs my hands in front and walks me to the admin office, where a female guard sits behind a counter.

"Get changed and come back to sign some paperwork," she says.

I'm uncuffed, and a stack of clothes—my clothes —is pushed toward me. I stand there, fucking dumbfounded, waiting for the punchline because this can't be real.

"Unless you'd rather stay? I'm sure we can work something out," she says.

"No. I'm good." I grab my clothes and quickly change in the bathroom, leaving the ugly ass jumpsuit on the floor. The weight of my cut on my shoulders feels fucking incredible, and I've never been happier to feel leather boots on my feet.

Back at the desk, the guard has me sign a bunch of shit I don't understand. Something about how being released doesn't make me innocent of the crime and how they can try me at a later date if more evidence is collected. It's a bunch of legal jargon I'll have to have my lawyer decipher later. All I know is they're letting me out, and I'm not about to question it.

"That's it. You're free to go." She hands me a plastic bag with my wallet, cellphone, and everything else they collected from me, then points at the exit.

"Thanks," I mutter and step outside.

I was only in jail for two weeks, but it felt longer than the fifteen years I served before this. The air is thick and stifling in the summer heat, but my lungs inhale it deeply anyway. Smells like freedom. Motherfucking freedom.

"You gonna stand there and sniff the air all day, or

can we get outta here?" Sin calls out from the parking lot.

It's then I notice all my brothers are here. Sin, Risk, Ruin, Tank, Rule, Dare, and Devil are straddling their bikes with big ass grins on their faces. Sin motions to the bike next to him. Aw, shit. They even brought my baby.

My smile can't be contained as I walk over, arms wide. "Someone care to explain how this happened?"

"Don't know, man. Got a call from the Sheriff. He said you were being released today and asked if one of us could pick you up. Thought it'd be better if we all picked you up." Sin hands me my helmet.

"The sheriff?" I ask, confused. Then it clicks. Talynn. She must be behind this.

"I don't know how he pulled this off."

"I don't know either, brother. But some things you don't question." Sin starts his bike, triggering the others to do the same. I strap on my dome and bring my baby to life, feeling her blessed vibration between my legs.

Ruin takes the lead, and we all follow. He must know I need a ride after being cooped up because we don't get back to the clubhouse for an hour, and by the time we do, my head is clear, and my soul is at rest.

I need to talk to Talynn, but it's the middle of the day, and she's probably working. Instead, I change into my work boots and seek out my other best friends.

"Hey, Sugar." I approach the brown horse, half an apple in hand. "You miss me?"

Her eyes go wide, and after snagging the apple from my palm, she stomps her foot and whinnies.

After spoiling all the beasts with treats and pets, I head back to my cabin and shower. I feel like a goddamn teenager with butterflies in my belly as I think about seeing Talynn. I don't know what kind of strings she had to pull, but fuck if I'm not happy she did.

I could probably find out by calling my public defender, but I wanna hear it from her lips. Then after she explains, I want to use those pouty lips for other things. She teased the fuck out of me by climbing on my lap when she came to see me in jail, and I deserve some payback. It wasn't fun walking back to my cell while trying to hide my erection. The blue balls that followed were even less fun.

Once the sun goes down, I figure she's probably home, so I mount my baby and ride over to her house. Pulling up, I notice her old truck is back in the driveway. She must've gotten it back with the unused cash. Her patrol car is here too, which means so is she.

I park, walk up the steps, and knock three times, interested to see how she pulled this off and hoping like hell that I won't get shot down.

She opens the door with a smile, but she clearly wasn't expecting me because it falls at the same time her eyes widen in surprise. "Colt?"

"They released me. Thought you had somethin' to do with it, but I'm guessin' I was wrong."

"I had no idea." Even stunned stupid, this woman is beautiful.

She must've only recently gotten home because her hair is still in a tight bun and her ugly brown uniform is on, though the heavy belt, black shoes, and badge are missing. Her shirt is untucked, and two buttons are undone at the top.

I hold up the envelope of paperwork. "I brought this, thought you might be able to make sense of it because Lord knows I can't."

"Sure. Yeah. Come in." She stands to the side for me to pass. Not exactly the homecoming I thought I'd get. "Can I get you some coffee, water, lemonade?"

"You got a beer?"

"Yeah. Actually, I could use one too." She disappears into the kitchen, and I sit on her vintage sofa.

Sitting on her end table is a stack of beer coasters. I snag one and tuck in my cut. I haven't had the chance to add to my collection lately. Wonder how long it'll take her to realize I've been stealing shit from her house since the first time I came here.

After setting the papers on the coffee table, I sit back and rest an ankle on my knee and wait.

"Here you go." She hands me a bottle of beer. It's not that I thought she'd jump my bones the second she saw me, but she's acting like she doesn't even know who I am.

"If you're busy or somethin', I can g—"

"No. Don't go. I'm sorry. I'm just shocked. I can't believe they let you go."

"It's fine. I get it. I'm shocked myself. Want to try and make heads or tails of this?" I point to the papers.

She sits down beside me and sets her beer on a coaster while she reads. I pop the top of her bottle before my own, then take a long swig. The cold, bubbly hops go down easy. I told myself I'd never take anything for granted after I got out of prison, but as the weeks went by, so did my appreciation for little things. I think this last stint was a good reminder.

"It basically says the prosecution was forced to drop the case because evidence went missin'. Have you called your lawyer?" she asks.

"No."

"Let's call and find out what happened."

I pull out my cell and dial her number, putting it on speed dial.

"This is Teresa," she answers.

"Hey, Teresa. This is Colton Masters."

"Mr. Masters, I knew I'd be hearing from you. I'm sorry I couldn't make it when they released you."

I lean forward, resting my forearms on my knees. "About that. Can you tell me what happened?"

"A couple days ago, I got a call from Sheriff Davis. He said there was an incident, and some evidence went missing. Apparently, the weapon they found on you was part of that. I met with the judge, who agreed it was material and dropped your case. It was all highly unusual."

"What if that evidence is found?" I ask.

"Then they'll charge you. That's what the paperwork you signed says. That just because they aren't now doesn't mean they can't or won't in the future. But the sheriff was adamant it's gone forever."

This is surreal. I'm used to shit coming my way, so this whole thing doesn't compute. I'd think my brothers were the ones to make the evidence disappear, except they would've told me. They had no idea why I was free either.

"That's wild," I say because what are the odds of that?

"I'd say so. My recommendation to you is to stay out of trouble. If you do, I don't foresee any problems. If there are, you have my number."

"Thanks."

"You're welcome."

I disconnect the line and glance over at Talynn, who's staring at the phone. "You good?"

"I think I know what happened."

"What's that?"

"Last time I talked to my dad, I told him to fix it. That was the day you were arrested, and I haven't spoken to him since."

"You know me gettin' arrested had nothing to do with him. That was all on me," I admit.

"I know, but it wasn't your fault when you were sixteen. He has a lot of making up to do."

I cup her cheek and smooth my thumb over her silky-smooth skin. "Love that you went to war with him for me, Bug, but hate that you're at odds with your daddy. He's your family."

"I was just so mad," she says through gritted teeth. "I always thought he was an honest, stand-up man. You know? The kind I compared every guy I dated to."

"Still think you should compare every man to him. He was protectin' his family. I'd do the same thing."

"How can you be so accepting of this? You lost over half your life." Her brown eyes glass over. Fuck me, I hate seeing her sad.

I drop my hand and rest it on my lap. "I can hate what he did—be pissed he took advantage of a kid—and still recognize he did what he thought was best for his boy. He lost one son that day, but he didn't want to lose two, and he saw an opportunity." I let my silence hang heavy between us for a moment. "I guess me and your dad made the same choice that day, to sacrifice one to save another. He sacrificed me, and I sacrificed myself. We both rolled the dice and crapped out."

Her shoulders curl. "This is all too much."

I chuckle humorously. "You're tellin' me."

"What are you going to do now?"

I lift my brows, gazing at her through my periphery. "Right now?"

"Right now, the rest of your life, whatever."

"I think Sheriff Davis and I need to have a talk. After that, I'd like to take this pretty girl I know out on a date. If she'll let me."

She rubs her hands down her polyester pants. "I don't know, Colt."

Ouch. Wasn't expecting that.

"What don't you know?"

"A lot of things. Even if we get past the whole *my dad sent you to prison* thing, there's still the fact that you're a Diamond King, and I'm a Sheriff's Deputy. How will that work?"

I shift to face her. "We don't have to solve all the world's problems right now. All I'm askin' for is a date."

"A date?" she repeats.

"Yeah. Take you out for dinner, a movie, that kind of thing."

She giggles. "I can't picture you goin' to a movie."

"Haven't been to one in a long ass time. Maybe I'll like it."

"A date," she says again, but it's a statement this time.

"How about Friday night? You free?" I stand up. As much as I want to stay and remind her how much she likes me—especially when I'm between her legs—I think we better take things slow.

"I don't have plans."

"Now you do."

CHAPTER 22
TALYNN

Driving to Daddy's house, my mind is overloaded with thoughts. I nearly had a heart attack when I saw Colt on my porch. My overactive imagination thought he broke out of prison and would ask me to run away with him.

I wouldn't have gone. Or would I?

I shake my head. That's stupid. Of course I wouldn't have.

The last couple weeks have been torture. Not a minute passed that I wasn't thinking about Colt. When I had breakfast, I'd wonder what he was eating. At night I'd wonder if he was thinking of me too.

Now he's free, and apparently, his gun went missing. It's not a coincidence. It can't be.

Which is why I'm going to Daddy's house. I don't

want any more lies or secrets between us. Never again. We're all that's left of our family, and it's time we started trusting each other.

I come to an abrupt halt in front of my childhood home. There's a For Sale sign posted on the lawn. What the hell? Taking a flier from the post, I scan it as I walk up the path to the front door.

Not bothering to knock, I storm in, crumpling the piece of paper. I find Daddy in his recliner—like always—beer in hand.

"You're selling my house?" I ask, fire in my tone.

"I'm selling *my* house." He pulls the lever to put his feet down. "Hi, Talynn. Nice to see you."

"Were you gonna tell me?"

"It's not like you've been approachable the last couple weeks." He folds his arms in front of him.

"You can't sell. I won't let you."

"Sorry to tell you, but it's not your choice."

"Why?"

"If you're gonna come in here demandin' answers, at least sit down so we can have a conversation like grown adults." He motions to the living room.

I stomp—not my finest moment—into the living room and sit down. Collapsing back into his recliner, he picks his beer up from the ground where he set it and takes a swig.

"So?" I demand.

"The house is too big for one person. It's time for another family to grow up here."

"But it's my house," I deadpan.

"I can't move on, Talynn. All I see when I walk in is your mom baking bread in the kitchen. Ben and Henry runnin' up and down the stairs. I can't escape it, and I need to. We both do."

He's right. I know he is. But it feels like a betrayal. Momma put everything she had into making this a home for her family.

"Where will you go?" I ask.

"Not sure yet. I have a real estate agent findin' a smaller place. Maybe out by the golf course in one of those condos."

I never paid much attention to the fact that the house is exactly as Momma left it. Nothing has changed. It must've been hard for him to be surrounded by the ghosts of the past for all these years.

"The golf course, huh? That'll be nice."

He settles back in his chair with a look of relief that I've given up my fight. "Might be. But you didn't come here to talk about that."

"I didn't."

"Why did you come?" he asks.

"Colton stopped by yesterday. They let him out because the gun went missin' from evidence."

"You don't say." The lack of shock tells me everything I need to know.

"You know anything about that?"

"Can't say I do, but I also can't say I'm disappointed."

"Daddy, you took a big risk. Are you sure it won't come back to you?" The last thing I need is for him to end up in prison next to Colt.

"I don't know what you're talking about. But if I did, then I'd tell you not to worry. Regardless of the stupid things I've done in my past, I'm not a stupid man. If I did something like that, I'd make sure it was clean."

A knock at the door has both of us tensing.

"Expecting anyone?" I ask.

"I'll get it."

I follow him to the front door to see the man we were just talking about standing on the porch. Colt's hands are tucked into his pockets, and his shoulders are drawn up.

"Sheriff," he says in greeting.

"Good to see you, son. What can I do for you?"

"I was hopin' to talk. Is this a good time?"

"Sure. Sure. Let's take a seat out here. It's a nice night." Daddy closes the door in my face, effectively blocking me from spying.

That was rude.

To kill time, I clean Daddy's kitchen and grill him some chicken and veggies for dinner later. After that, I pick up the living room. Then the dining room. It isn't until I'm washing all the windows that the door opens, and Daddy walks in, looking worn out. He's not an emotional man, so all this talking is draining on him.

"How'd it go?"

"Good. I think."

I set the window cleaner on the dining room table. "What do you mean, good?"

"Jesus Almighty, Talynn. We talked, and now he's gone." He settles into his recliner, kicking his feet up. Picking up his beer again, he takes a swig and winces. "Grab me a cold beer, would ya?"

"He's gone?" I ask.

"Said he had shit to do."

"Oh." I get a fresh bottle out of the fridge and hand it to him. "Was he okay?"

"Wouldn't say that. He was pissed at me. Rightfully so. But we cleared the air." He peers over at me. "He seems to be fond of you."

My cheeks heat. "What makes you think that?"

"Just a gut feeling."

Butterflies flutter around my tummy. I've never felt like this before. Not even when Sam Olson asked to kiss me after school in seventh grade. And it's over a man I have no business being with.

"Yeah, but did he say anything?"

"He didn't ask for your hand in marriage, if that's what you think." He takes a swig of beer to hide his smile. "But he did say he was takin' you on a date Friday."

"What do you think about that?" I ask.

"I think I saw how you looked at him when you were just a kid. Things got messed up along the way—there's been a lot of pain and sufferin'—but that's behind you now, and you still look at him the same way. That says somethin'."

"I don't look at him in any sorta way."

"You were droolin' all over yourself when you saw him on the porch just now," he teases.

I wipe the corner of my mouth. "Liar."

After the heaviness of the last few weeks, it feels good to joke around. I've missed Daddy, and I'm glad he worked things out with Colton. It makes it easier for me to move on from all this.

His smile fades. "It takes a special man to come here and forgive me. I don't deserve it."

I could placate him and tell him it's okay and everyone makes mistakes, but what he did was beyond terrible.

"You're right. You don't deserve it. I get why you did it, but it's inexcusable."

"I always prided myself on having integrity. Built my whole career on it. Then I saw my boy lying on the ground in a pool of his own blood"—his voice cracks, and he clears his throat—"and I did a lot of things I'm not proud of. Worse than that, it was all for nothin' because I still lost the kid I was tryin' to save. I don't know what kind of man that makes me, but there hasn't been a day since then that I've been proud of myself, and I'll die with that disappointment."

I can't clear his conscience; it's not me he wronged, not really. But I can show him unconditional love. I bend over and hug him with all I am.

"Love you, Daddy."

"Love you too."

My room is a disaster. Clothes are piled high on my bed and scattered all over my floor, and I still can't figure out what to wear. Since I have no idea where we're going, I'm not sure if I should keep it casual or dress up.

He's due to arrive any minute, and I'm still in my underwear.

I shriek when there's a knock on my door. *No, no, no.* He can't be here already. Throwing on my robe, I look through the peephole. It's him. Damn it. I scowl when I open the door.

"Skippin' right to dessert, I see," he says, eyeing me up and down.

"No, I just don't know what to. . ." My mouth goes dry, making speaking impossible. This man looks good enough to eat. His pressed Wranglers are tight in all the right places, and his short-sleeve white tee hugs his muscled arms, leaving his veined forearms on display. He has on the leather cut he always wears and motorcycle boots. The perfect mix of honorable cowboy and dangerous biker.

"You okay?" He smirks.

"I'm fine. Come on in. I'll just be a minute." I

motion to the living room as I pass by, but he doesn't take the hint. Instead, he follows me to my room. "Colt, I'm changin'."

"I know." He grabs the tie of my robe and rips it open, exposing me to him. Licking his lips, he takes a step back while his eyes eat me up.

Goosebumps spread across my skin, yet I'm burning up. I don't own lingerie, so I'm wearing basic white undies and a sheer white bra. It's nothing special, yet the way he's looking at me tells me he thinks it is.

"What are you doin'? We have a date," I say dumbly.

"Plan's changed. We're staying in." He wraps his strong arms around my waist and lifts me up. I lock my legs around his waist and lower my lips to his.

This works out better for me. Now I won't have to choose an outfit.

My core throbs as he shoves me against the wall, placing a hand behind my head a second before I hit. *How thoughtful.* That hand slides down my body, cupping my breast roughly.

"Never thought I'd get another chance to hear you scream my name," he grinds out.

"Cute you think you have that power over me," I tease.

He lifts a challenging brow. "Wanna make a bet?"

"What are the terms?"

"If I win"—he nips my lower lip—"you gotta start callin' me Crow."

He attacks my neck, licking and sucking while grinding his erection against my sensitive core.

"And if I win?" I breathe out.

"Then I'll keep givin' you orgasms until you *do* scream my name." He tugs down the cup of my bra and pinches my nipple.

"It's a bet."

He growls and carries me over to the bed, where he tosses me onto my back. "On your knees and grip that headboard."

Letting my robe fall away, I push clothes off my bed as I go, excitement bubbling throughout my body. My need for him is bone-deep. Every inch of me craves his touch, his kisses, his attention.

I place my hands on the headboard and peer over my shoulder as he toes off his boots, an animalistic gleam in his eyes. "You're beautiful, Bug. So fuckin' gorgeous, it hurts."

A blush spreads across my cheeks and down my chest. God, what this man does to me.

His cut comes off next, which he reverently deposits on my reading chair in the corner. I know the club means a lot to him; it's probably why he wants me to call him Crow. All he had to do was ask and I would, but this bet makes things so much more fun.

He tears off his belt, followed by his T-shirt. I didn't get that good of a look at him last time we were together, so I utilize this time wisely, taking in every muscle, every patch of hair, and spend a lot of time focused on the deep V leading down his hips.

I nearly come on the spot when he loses his pants and boxers, remembering how talented his rock-hard cock is. He strokes himself as he stalks toward me and climbs on the bed.

With a smack on my ass, he says, "Ready to lose our bet?"

"I'm ready to see you try."

CHAPTER 23
CROW

"You look so innocent in granny panties," I say into her ear, rubbing my cock between the cheeks of her ass. "But I know the truth."

"I wanted to be comfortable."

"I like 'em." Gripping the side of her panties, I tear them at the seam. She gasps, peering over her shoulder at me. I move to the other side and do the same, then pull them clean off. "But I like 'em even more on the ground."

Moving onto her bra, I unclasp it at her back and push it down her arms. She tosses it to the side. Her body is trembling with anticipation, making my cock ache. I love seeing the physical signs of her want for me.

Pushing her hair over her shoulder, I take my time

placing open-mouthed kisses along her shoulders and up her neck, grinning when goosebumps pop up in my wake.

"You ready for me, Bug?" I wrap an arm around her hips and pull back, popping her ass out. Reaching between her legs, I'm surprised to feel bare skin. "Why'd you shave?"

"It's more sanitary?" she says as though it's a question.

"No, it's not."

"I thought you'd like it," she tries again.

"No more shaving. You can trim all you want, but I like knowin' I'm fuckin' a grown woman." I spread her lips and drag a finger through her arousal.

"No shaving." She moans. "Got it."

"You're drippin' down my finger, and I've barely touched you." I bite down on her earlobe, giving it a tug. "I'm so winnin' this bet."

I pull away and knead the globes of her ass, warming her up before I slap each one. She gasps, her grip on the wooden headboard tightening.

"Do it again," she whispers, arching her back so her ass sticks out even more.

Fuck me. Those words are like kerosene, lighting the fire within me.

Smack. Smack.

"Wish you could see how beautiful you look like this," I say, wrapping my body around hers. I grip the base of her throat with one hand, and with the other, I cup her heavy breast. "Never wanted anything more than I want you."

"Then take me. Do it now. Please."

Releasing her, I line my cock up at her entrance and push inside with a groan of pleasure. I missed out on so much being locked up, but none of it pisses me off more than knowing I was missing out on this. Missing out on fucking this woman day and night.

There's not a doubt in my mind that if things had been different, we would've been together long before now. The world tried to keep us apart, fuck did it try, but she and I are a force of nature.

With my hands on her hips, I fuck her good and hard, making sure she feels me in places she won't soon forget. With every thrust forward, she pushes back, filling the silence with the sound of our flesh slapping together.

My balls tighten, reminding me I have the stamina of a sixteen-year-old. *Fuck that*.

"Turn around," I say. It takes everything in me to pull out and lie down. "Get on top. Wanna see those tits bounce."

She straddles me, taking my cock in hand and

positioning me. She sinks down slowly, her eyes rolling back as she does. I grip the back of her neck and pull her to me for a kiss, plunging my tongue into her mouth to taste her. Her hips rock, and her breasts rub up and down my chest as I suck on her lips.

This isn't helping. Matter of fact, my situation is growing more urgent. Need to get her off, and I need to do it now.

I release her, and she sits back up, her hands moving to my chest for purchase. Her skin is beautifully flushed, and her brown hair is wild. The buttoned-up version of her is gone, and the woman underneath is exposed. I'm damn lucky to be the one who gets to see her like this.

She grinds back and forth, seeking her pleasure while I play with her tits, flicking her nipples and tugging on them. Her mouth falls open, and I know she's close.

"Be a good girl and come all over my cock. Wanna feel you."

Her grip on my dick tightens, and her movements get rougher, more intense. It's time for me to take over. I lift my hips and thrust up into her over and over, reaching between her legs until I find her swollen clit. I rub back and forth while I fuck her from below.

"Oh God," she croaks right before she explodes.

She holds my gaze, her pupils blown as her hips tuck, and she clenches down on me with a vice-like grip.

"Colton. Fuck. Yes," she cries.

I couldn't hold back my orgasm if I tried. Gritting my teeth, I give her everything I have. An inferno spreads through me, and I come so hard, the world could crash down around us, and I wouldn't know.

"Mine. Mine. Mine. You're mine," I grit out as I coat her insides with my cum.

Slowly, everything comes back into focus as she works us down from our high with slow, gentle movements. Her hands run up and down my body, her face lax and her eyes soft.

Eventually, she collapses on top of me, and I wrap my arms around her. Our slick skin sticks together as I hold her tight, never wanting to let go. Not ever.

"Love you, Bug," I say. And maybe it's too soon and overly sentimental, but I don't fucking care.

Her head pops up, and our eyes meet. "You do?"

"With everythin' I am." Seeing her hesitation, I add, "Don't have to say it back. That's not why I told you."

"I've been in love with you since I was twelve.

My feelings got mixed up there for a while, but the second I learned the truth, it all came back."

"You have no idea how happy it makes me to hear you say that." I hug her to me again. We lie like this for a long minute until my cock slips out and my cum drips from her cunt. "We need a shower."

"Ooh, shower sex. Sounds fun."

My eyes peel open to a ray of sunshine hitting me right in the face. I block it with a hand, blinking as I get my bearings. Tucked to my side is a still naked Talynn.

This must be what heaven feels like.

I carefully slide my arm out from under her and get up, trying not to wake her but failing.

"What time is it?" She yawns, stretching her arms overhead. The blanket slips, falling below her perky tits covered in love bites.

We never did make it out of the house last night. We fucked again in the shower, and she made us dinner, followed by more fucking. We passed out right before the sun came up, exhausted and happy.

I glance at my phone. "Ten."

"Dang. I need to get up and get ready for work."

Sliding back in bed, I climb on top of her, holding myself up with my hands on either side of her. "Call in sick."

"Your pecker is gonna fall off if I don't get some space between us for a few hours." She giggles.

"My pecker is just fine, thank you very much." To prove my point, I press my already hard cock against her.

She runs her hands in my hair. "I've missed too much work lately."

"Miss more." I dip down and kiss her neck, eliciting a shiver.

"Tempting, but no can do." She slips out from underneath me.

Rolling onto my side, I grumble something about how dumb work is while she pulls a pressed uniform from her closet.

"Stay at my place tonight," I say, propping my head up on a hand.

She blinks, freezing in place. "On the ranch? I don't think so."

"Why not?"

"How bad would it look for a sheriff's deputy to be hanging out with outlaws?" She shakes her head. "Absolutely not."

Her adamance irks me to no end. Sure, we aren't exactly law-abiding citizens, but we do a lot to keep this town safe. It more than makes up for our extracurricular earnings.

"So that's how it's gonna be from now on? If I wanna see you, I gotta come here?" I ask.

"Well, yeah." She says it like it's a given.

It's not a fucking given.

"Those men are my brothers. That club is my home."

She pulls on another pair of white panties, momentarily distracting me. They shouldn't be sexy but fuck if I find them that way.

"I'm sorry, Colt—"

"Crow," I correct. I won that bet fair and square.

She rolls her eyes. "I'm sorry, *Crow*, but I need to think of my career. I want to be Sheriff someday like my daddy, and I can't be associated with the club."

"People are gonna see you with me."

"How?" She fastens her bra in place. *Such a shame.*

"When we go out."

"Where are we gonna go?"

"You were ready to go on a date with me last night."

"Well, yeah. But I assumed we'd be going out of town since there's not much to do in Diamond."

I'm heated now, my temper start to boil. Getting out of bed, I quickly pull my jeans and T-shirt on. "That ain't gonna work for me, Bug. If you're with me, you gotta be *with* me. On my arm, on the back of my bike, at the fuckin' Get Go."

"It's not like you hang out around here anyway. I know you've been avoiding town since the incident at the *Get Go*," she sasses. "It'll be even worse for you now that everyone knows you were arrested again."

Of course the kindergarten cop is out there blabbing about arresting me.

I run a hand through my hair. "I don't give a shit what they think of me. You know why?"

"Why?" She buttons her poop brown shirt. As she slips each button into the loop, I see the Talynn from last night disappearing.

"They don't know me. They're a bunch of judgmental assholes who have nothing better to do than cast stones."

"Not all of them."

This time, I'm the one rolling my eyes. "The only people who matter to me are the ones I matter to. My brothers."

"That's it, huh? No one else?" She throws her arms in the air.

"And you." I crowd her space, tipping her chin up to look at me. "You matter a whole helluva lot to me, and I want you in my life. But I'm a package deal. If you can't accept me for who I am, we have no future."

Fuck if that doesn't hurt to say, but it's the God's honest truth. My club took me in when everyone else turned their back on me. I'll die before I turn my back on them.

"I don't know, Colt."

"Crow," I correct again.

She sighs. "I need time to think."

I cup her cheeks and kiss her good and hard. "Don't think too long."

CHAPTER 24
TALYNN

"God, you're so depressed, you're bumming me out," Sarah says, stirring her coffee.

"I'm sorry. I just have a lot on my mind."

It's been a week since Colt was in my bed. I didn't mean for it to take me this long to decide what to do, but work was busy, and I've been helping Daddy pack up. They're lame excuses, but they're what I'm telling myself because I honestly don't know what to do.

Sarah sets her spoon down. "Talk. Tell me what's got you down."

"Well, I told you Colton and I were going to date."

"I take it things aren't going well?"

"They were going *really* well." I smile, thinking about our one perfect night.

"Dish. I wanna hear all about it."

"We didn't even make it out of my house."

"Go on." She gestures with her hands for me to continue.

"He's intense. When we're *together*, it feels like he's everywhere at once. He steals my breath and makes me feel beautiful and sexy. I've never felt like this before. Not even close."

"Wow. Maybe you should take me with you to the Diamond Kings Ranch. I could use a little of that."

"That's the thing. The mornin' after, he asked me to stay the night at his place, but I don't think that's appropriate given my job," I say.

"You're a deputy, not a saint. You're allowed to have a life. As long as they're not murderin' people, sellin' drugs, or whatever they do over there, right in front of you, you have plausible deniability, right?"

I pin her with a look. "The people in this town don't even know what *plausible deniability* is."

"You're probably right. So now what? You break up?" Sarah has a way of simplifying even the most complex issues.

"I don't want to." I peel the paper from my muffin. "I have feelings for him. Deep feelings."

"You love him?" she asks with a mouthful of scone.

"I think I do."

"Holy shit, Tal," she yells, gaining disapproving looks from the entire café. "Sorry!" She lowers her voice. "Holy shit, Tal."

"You're ridiculous."

She waves me off. "Clearly, you need some perspective, and as your best friend, I'm happy to deliver it to you."

I exhale. "Okay, let's hear it."

"You have always been untouchable. Sure, you dated a few guys, but you could take 'em or leave 'em. There's only been one person in this whole world that's turned you to mush." Her brows and chin raise. "Colton fuckin' Masters. Ever since Henry brought him to your house when you were a little girl, you've only had eyes for him. When everything went down, it broke your heart to think the only guy you've ever put on a pedestal—other than your daddy—could do something like that. It destroyed you. You became this sad, bitter person who didn't trust anyone."

I scowl, picking off chunks of my muffin and tossing them on the table. I'll clean it up when we leave. I just need to be destructive right now.

"Don't give me that look, you know you have

been. And no one blamed you because you lost Ben and your momma. Two people you loved with your whole heart."

"I miss them," I say.

"I know you do. Which is why you got away with being—I'm just going to say it—dull."

"Sarah!"

"Sorry, babe. We both know it's true. The second Colt came back to town, you came to life. You were mostly angry and hostile, but still. You were showin' emotions other than indifference. I watched as all that pent-up rage changed into something else, and now today, you're saying things like 'he steals your breath,' and you're saying them with a smile on your face." Her eyes widen, her mouth drops open, and she leans back into her chair. "That's an improvement, babe."

"You're telling me things I already know."

"Then you already know the answer. You deserve to be happy, despite this town. Sure, there'll be an uproar, and everyone will gossip for a month or so, but then Mr. Fernley will drive his tractor into Mr. Conley's barn, drunk off his ass." She looks over my shoulder and waves. "Hi, Mr. Fernley."

I glance back and see the old coot walking into the diner and smile.

Focusing back on me, she continues, "And everyone will forget all about you and focus on his alcoholism."

"You think?"

"I know."

"Maybe you're right, but I should talk about all this with my dad before decidin', right?"

"Talynn Davis," she reprimands. "Stop living your life for other people and go get your man."

I slip into the wide-leg jeans I sporadically sewed smiley face patches on and pair them with a white crochet tank, some chunky sandals, and a crystal necklace. I take one last glance at myself in the mirror before getting in my truck and heading for Diamond Kings Ranch.

My palms are so sweaty that they slip and slide over my steering wheel as I make the fifteen-minute drive. My nerves flare, and I might throw up, but I keep going. I can do this.

Parking in front of his cabin, I'm worried he might not be here, but he steps onto the small porch, likely hearing my old truck pull up. He crosses his arms and leans against the door jamb, face stoic.

Reluctantly, I hop out and walk around to stand in front of him. "Hey."

"Hi."

"Can we talk?"

"You sure you don't wanna think on it for a few months?" he asks.

"It's only been two weeks, don't be dramatic."

"Come on in." He holds the door open for me.

Things have changed a little since I was here last. There are a few pictures of him with other men in leather vests—I'm assuming his *brothers*—hanging on the wood-paneled walls, and there's a TV mounted in front of the love seat and a coat rack by the door.

"Take a seat. You want somethin' to drink?"

"I'll take a beer if you have it." I could use some alcoholic lubrication to move this conversation along.

Instead of sitting down, I follow him into the small kitchen, wanting to see if he's decorated in there too. A collection of trinkets on the windowsill catches my attention. I move closer to check it out, but he blocks my path.

"Here you go." He thrusts a beer in my direction.

"Thanks." I try to bypass him, but he sidesteps, blocking me again. "What's on the windowsill?"

"Nothin'. Come on, let's talk in the living room."

"No, I want to see."

"It's nothin'," he argues, but there's a wrinkle in his forehead like he's nervous.

I move over as though I've given up and will follow him, but the second he steps forward, I slink past him and dash to the window. There's a coaster, a bird figurine, a seashell soap, a small, framed picture of Henry, Ben, Colt, and me in the front yard of my childhood home, and a peace sign necklace.

"Did you steal all of this?" I ask, collecting all my things.

"I wouldn't say steal," he says, shrugging. "More like borrowed."

"Why?"

"It's my crow's nest."

"Crow's nest?"

"You know how crows see shiny things and bring them back to their nest."

"And you're a crow?"

His answer is to point to the name patch on his vest. "Crow."

"You know that's a myth, right?"

"How would you know?" He takes my stuff from my hands and sets it back on the sill.

"I read about it in college." I study him, confused why he would do something like this. It's so odd.

Then it hits me. My home is full of memories. Everywhere you look, I have something that reminds me of a certain time in my life. It's what comforts me when I'm sad or feeling alone. All I have to do is look around, and I'm reminded of all the love and fun I've had throughout the years.

Colton doesn't have that. He left prison with nothing.

"Babe," I say, cupping his cheeks.

"Babe? You never called me that before." His hands go to my waist.

I ignore that for now because I'm as shocked as he is. I've never called *anyone* that.

"You needed things to remind you of me," I say.

"Don't get all mushy about it." It's hard to tell with all the scruff he's grown the last two weeks and his tanned skin from working outside, but if I'm not mistaken, his cheeks pink up.

"It is mushy. And sweet." I lift onto my toes and give him a chaste kiss. "You can keep it."

"I was plannin' on that anyway." He smirks.

Scratching my nails through his beard, I say, "I'm sorry it took me so long."

He holds me at arm's distance. "Does this mean you're choosin' me?"

"Yeah, babe. I'm choosing you."

"Hot damn." He throws a shoulder into my hips, lifting me up.

"What are you doing?"

"Takin' my woman to bed." He turns and stomps to his bedroom.

"We haven't talked," I whine, but I'm laughing, pounding fists on his ass.

"Talk later. Fuck now." He sets me on my feet in front of his bed.

I laugh as he gets on one knee and lifts my foot onto it, fumbling with the buckle on my sandal. Once that's off, he moves to the next.

"Why aren't you helpin' me? Get naked, woman." He stands and spins me around, trying to figure out how to untie my crocheted top. It's too funny to watch him struggle, so I stand limply as he works. "Are you not feelin' the urgency I am?"

"I like you undressing me." My top falls to the ground, leaving me bare-chested and sidetracking him.

He draws me to him, a hand on my breast. "Missed these."

"They missed you too."

He dips down to kiss me, his overgrown beard chaffing my chin, but I couldn't care less. He licks the seam of my lips, and I open for him, allowing his tongue to plunge inside and explore while he plucks at my nipples.

"Stop distractin' me," he says, against my lips, moving his hands down to the button on my pants.

He unzips them and lowers to his knees, working them and my panties down my thighs, putting him at eye level with my pussy that I haven't shaved since we were together last.

"Now this is what I like." He grips my hips and buries his face against me, inhaling.

"What are you—" My eyes roll back into my head when he tosses my leg over his shoulder and sweeps his tongue up my slit.

I brace myself with a hand on his head as he eats me out, licking and sucking. A finger enters me, hooking so it hits me in the perfect spot, and I nearly go cross-eyed with pleasure. One finger becomes two as he strokes me from the inside while latching onto my clit and sucking.

"I'm comin', Crow. Oh God, just like that." I hold him to me, grinding against his face like the hussy he makes me.

My thighs quiver and my heart races as overwhelming pleasure explodes from my core. Holy crap that felt good.

His beard is glistening, and he's sporting a devilish smile when he comes up for air. He strips off his cut, placing it on his dresser before tugging off his shirt, using it to wipe his face. *Barbarian*.

"Fuck, I missed you," he says, pushing down his pants. His cock stands proud, the tip already leaking pre-cum. My mouth waters, and I slide off the bed and sink to my knees. He pinches my chin and tilts my head up. "Whatcha doin' down there, Bug?"

"Don't call me that when I'm eye level with your dick."

"Why?"

"It makes me sound like a child."

He chuckles. "Trust me, *Bug*, I know you're all woman. You still good with rough?"

I lick my lips. The few times I've performed oral, it wasn't my idea, and I didn't enjoy it. But looking at his angry red tip dripping with pearly fluid, I want nothing more than to have him in my mouth.

"Do your best," I challenge.

CHAPTER 25
CROW

I put on a good show of knowing what the hell I'm doing, but I've never had my cock sucked before, and the thought alone is bringing me close to blowing. What'll happen when her hot mouth is wrapped around me?

Time to find out.

"Good girl," I say, fisting my cock and painting her lips with pre-cum.

Her tongue traces the path I left, and she hums. *God help me with this woman.*

She takes me in hand and licks the sensitive underside of my shaft, all the way to my balls, where she sucks one into her mouth, keeping her eyes locked on mine.

"Fuuuuck," I groan, my head lulling back.

Releasing it with a *pop*, she kisses her way back to my tip and opens wide, taking me down her throat. It's heaven—angels singing, white light shining heaven. She bobs up and down, using her tight fist to stroke what she can't fit.

"Stick out your tongue," I order, gathering her hair into a ponytail. With her in control like this, I might come before getting inside her. No, not happening. I need to reign it in and be the one to decide how this is gonna go.

She releases me and rests her hands on her thighs, tongue out and flat. I guide her down my length until I hit the back of her throat, and she gags, then I pull back out and do it all over again.

"You look so fuckin' beautiful on your knees, doin' all you can to please me." I pick up the pace, not giving her a break before pushing back in.

Saliva and pre-cum pool at the corner of her mouth as I fuck it. The collection gets bigger and bigger until it's running down her chin, eventually landing on her teardrop tits. She reaches up and smears it into her skin, fondling her breasts.

It's dirty and sexy and raunchy and everything in-between. My balls draw up, wanting so bad to come down her throat. But not now. Not this time.

I pull out. "Need to be inside your pussy. Hop up onto the bed."

She lifts onto the edge of the mattress—chest heaving, lips swollen, eyes shining, and hair mussed. A vision of sex and sin. I give her a little push, and she falls onto her back.

Her hair is splayed around her, her arms spread out to the side, and she's got her lust-filled eyes on me. I can't help but think about how far we've come and how much forgiving we've both done to get here. Our paths were not easy but fucking look at us now.

It's not gonna be easy. We still got shit to work out, but goddamn it, it'll be worth it. I lean over and kiss her, keeping my eyes open because I'm still not sure this is real.

"Love you, Bug," I say as I pull away.

"I love you too, Crow."

Today's the first time she's called me that on her own, and it validates everything I've done to forget my past. Colton was a stupid sixteen-year-old kid who thought he was doing right but ended up fucking himself in every way possible. Crow is a grown man with faults but is trying his best.

"Gonna fuck you now."

"I think that would be best." She smirks.

Talynn is different too. The first version I met was

uptight and resentful. But the version who showed up at my door today is light and sassy.

And so goddamn sexy.

I lift her legs onto my shoulders and tug her by the thighs until her ass is off the edge of the mattress. With my left hand, I reach up and stroke her soft calf. With my right, I grip my shaft and drag the head of my cock up and down her slit.

"You have the prettiest pussy," I say.

Each time we've been together, there was a rushed frenzy behind it, as though we both knew it wouldn't last. This time is different. I don't have to hurry because she's not going anywhere.

I push in further and spread her open with my fingers. "And look at this clit."

"Crow," she whines, squirming as she tries to take me deeper.

I slap her cunt, making her gasp in surprise. "I want to look at you, study you, commit you to memory."

"But I need you."

I grin. "Be patient."

Rubbing at her little nub, I push in another inch and stop, marveling at how inner lips curl around me. Her clit swells as I continue to give it attention.

Talynn writhes, fisting the sheets at her side, her eyes closed and lips parted as her breath picks up.

"What a greedy cunt. Look at how you're suckin' me in." I thrust in more, and she bears down, gripping me so good.

All the blood drains from my head and rushes to my cock. My own patience slips, and I push in all the way, my balls hitting her ass.

"Yes," she hisses.

I grip her by the front of her thighs and fuck her properly. Her heels dig into my shoulders, and she tilts her pelvis so I'm hitting her right where she needs it. My eyes lock onto her bouncing tits with rosy, puckered nipples. Licking my lips, I stop fucking her to lean over and suck one into my mouth.

This position nearly bends her in half, pushing my cock in to the hilt, but my girl's bendy and doesn't mind. She arches her back as much as she can and weaves her hands in my hair, holding me to her breasts as I lick, bite, and suck. Her skin smells sweet and tastes even better.

"Can't get enough of you, Bug. Never fuckin' will," I murmur against her tit.

"You better not."

Standing back up, I regain my pace, the sound of our skin slapping and our panting breaths reverberating through the cabin. The fire in me burns brighter, threatening to make me implode. I part her folds, gathering saliva in my mouth, and spit on her clit to use as lube. With my palm splayed on her soft lower belly, I rub my thumb against her swollen bud.

"Crow!" she cries out. "Yes. Just like that."

Her grip on my cock tightens, and I pick up my pace, clenching my jaw as I fuck her harder. She pushes up onto her elbows, changing the angle, her mouth dropping open and her eyes rolling back into her head. Jesus fucking Christ. The look of pure pleasure as she spasms around me sends me over the cliff.

I grip the front of her thighs again, digging my fingers into her flesh to push in deep and hold myself there. My entire body seems to vibrate, and blood rushes in my ears as I coat her inner walls with my seed, muttering unintelligibly about what a good girl she is and how much I fucking love her.

She holds my gaze through it all, her eyes saying everything I need to hear.

Then it's over, and the euphoria sets in. I laugh as I kiss each of her calves before setting her feet on the edge of the bed. Wincing, I pull out. Her pussy is still spasming, and as I watch, my cum leaks from her and down to her ass. I gather it up with a finger and push it back where it belongs.

Someday, I'll convince her to come off birth control, and I'll put our baby in her womb. I can't fucking wait to give us both back the family we lost on a hot day in July twenty years ago. It's a do-over I don't deserve but fuck if I won't take it anyway.

"Caveman," she says with a smile.

"You love me." I flop down next to her, snaking a hand under her head and bringing her close.

"More than you'll ever know."

"Hide your guns and drugs. The cops are here," Ruin shouts as we walk into the clubhouse.

"Shut up," I say, laughing despite Talynn's wide-eyed expression. I wrap an arm around her shoulders and pull her in to kiss her temple. "He's kiddin', Bug."

The clubhouse is a converted barn with round tables, chairs, and pool tables lined up to our right. On the opposite side is a long bar where my brothers are congregated, having a beer.

"Guys, this is Talynn," I call out.

They return hesitant greetings. It's clear having Talynn here is putting them on edge, but they'll have to get used to it because she's not going anywhere.

"Tal, this is Ruin, the club president."

"Hi, Ruin." Tal holds out her hand. He stares at it for a long minute before turning on his barstool and taking it.

"Your dad's the sheriff, right?"

"He is," she says proudly.

"This gonna be a problem, Crow?" One brow arches.

"It won't." Talynn's tone is confident and strong, making me proud as fuck.

"Good. You want a beer?" he offers.

"No," I interject. "We have plans. Just wanted y'all to meet my woman."

"Your woman, huh?" Sin asks.

"Tal, this is Sin, the VP."

"Nice to meet you." She smiles.

"Aw, don't be shy." Sin stands and hooks an arm around my neck. "I'm his best friend."

I struggle out of his hold and push him away playfully. "You think too much of yourself."

"We braid each other's hair and paint each other's toenails every night." Sin pounds me on the back.

"Asshole."

Talynn laughs at the interaction. It fills me with

pride that she's giving the guys a fair shake. If she likes them, it'll make my life so much easier.

"We're goin' ridin'," I say and take Talynn's hand, leading her to the door.

"We are?" she asks.

"Yep."

"I'm wearin' wedges." She lifts her foot, and I frown. Shit. Didn't think about footwear. "Oh, wait. I have a pair of boots in my truck."

After a stop-off for a shoe change, I lead her to the garage where we keep our bikes.

"When you said we were riding, I thought you meant on horses," she says.

"Nope." I hand her a helmet.

She eyes my baby. "I've never ridden on a motorcycle."

"Kind of like ridin' a horse."

She makes no move to put the helmet on, so I take it from her and set it on her head before buckling it carefully under her chin.

"I don't know. Aren't these things dangerous?"

"You're a cop. You're in danger every day." I straddle the bike and bring it to life.

"That's different," she shouts.

"You're right. You're safer on my bike. Get on."

"Can't we take the horses instead?"

I roll my eyes. "Get on the bike, Talynn."

"I've been to my share of motorcycle accidents. They never fair well for the rider."

"Get your ass on my bike." My tone brooks no argument but still, she falters. "Swear to God, Bug. You don't get on this bike right now, I'll spank your ass raw."

She startles and inches closer before swinging her leg over and settling behind me with her hands on my hips. That won't do, so I grip her by the wrists and tug her so close that her breasts press against my back. *Better*.

I start out slow, letting her get a feel for things until we reach the highway, then I take off. Her hold around me tightens, bringing a smile to my face. Feels fucking incredible to have her behind me while we cruise.

Getting brave, she reaches under my cut and lets her hands wander up and down my torso. I reach down and stroke her thigh for the briefest second before putting it back on the handlebar so she doesn't freak out.

We ride out to an area I know where there's a huge pond and some trees. I hope she finds it romantic, though I'm not even sure I know what that means. Dad had only started to talk to me about girls when I was locked up, and I'm certain taking advice from a fifty-year-old cellmate who's pen pals with a chick named Christa isn't a good idea. If it were, I'd be sending Talynn dick pics on the daily.

After an hour's drive, I park in the lot and help Tal off the bike. "How was it?"

"Amazin'. It's a lot more fun than I thought it would be. After I got over my fear of becoming roadkill." She unclips her helmet and sets it on the seat.

"Come on. Thought we could take a walk around the pond and have that talk you've been wantin'." I take her hand and guide her to the trail.

The sun is setting, so the temp has cooled enough to not melt your skin off your bones, and there's a slight breeze that feels good against my sweaty skin. The pond is pretty, but I can't keep my eyes off Tal.

"Things might get tricky between us," she says, breaking the silence. "But I don't want my job to come between us."

"I don't want my job to either."

"I don't want to know about your club business."

"Good. I don't want to tell you about it." I stroke my thumb over her hand.

"If something's going on, I trust you won't invite me to the clubhouse."

"That's a given."

She stops, facing me. "Is this a mistake?"

I push a piece of hair off her cheek. "We're not a mistake, Bug. We're a given. Like summer nights and fireflies. But you need to promise if somethin' isn't workin' for you, you talk to me about it and not run away."

"I will." Her brown eyes shine with happiness.

"Plus, we won't be stayin' at the ranch much."

"Why not?" she asks.

"Because I'm movin' in with you."

Her head tilts. "When did we decide this?"

"*We* didn't decide shit. While you were ignorin' me the last two weeks, I had some time to think, and I decided I like the idea of livin' together. Since we can't move into my place, yours'll do."

"Oh yeah?" Her brows lift, but she's smiling. She likes the idea. Good.

"Yeah." I hook an arm around her neck and keep walking, her arm going naturally around my waist. "We'll be just fine."

The End

ABOUT THE AUTHOR

Misty Walker is a USA Today Bestselling contemporary romance author. Her novels range between sweet and steamy to dark and delicious. Representation is important in her writing, so readers can expect a range of ethnicities and sexualities.

If you'd like to keep up to date on all her future releases, please sign up for her newsletter on her website, authormistywalker.com. You can also order a signed paperback of this book, or any of her releases, there.

Turn the page for a list of all of Misty Walker's books.

ALSO BY MISTY WALKER

Standalones:

Vindicated

Conversion (also available on audio)

Cop-Out

Crow's Scorn: Diamond Kings MC

Royal Bastards: Reno, NV:

Birdie's Biker (also available on audio)

Truly's Biker

Bexley's Biker

Riley's Biker

Petra's Bikers

Brigs Ferry Bay Series:

Kian's Focus (also available on audio)

Adler's Hart

Leif's Serenity

Doctor Daddy

Brigs Ferry Bay Omnibus

ACKNOWLEDGMENTS

Kristi, what self-help book do I need the most?

Ty-bot, thank you for being my safe place to land.

Ariadna, Sarah, Sara, Elizabeth, Lauren, and Jayce, thank you for being my beta team. I'm equally grateful and mortified that you see me in my rawest form and continue to stay!

Diana, thank you for being as excited about my ideas as I am!

Molly Whitman, you work as hard on my books as I do. Thank you!!

Mom, you are stronger than you'll ever know and tougher than any heroine I could ever write.

To my readers & my reader group, Misty Walker's Thirsty Readers, thank you the most! You guys rock my world and motivate me to keep writing. I love nothing more than to get your messages and read your reviews. It's a great big book world, but you choose to read my books, and that means everything.

Lorelai and Mabel, your mom writes dirty books and you're still proud of me. I love you.

Made in the USA
Middletown, DE
07 November 2023